THE BUDS OF BALLYBUNION

The Buds of Ballybunion

A PLAY IN THREE ACTS

JOHN B. KEANE

THE MERCIER PRESS
DUBLIN and CORK

The Mercier Press Limited
4 Bridge Street, Cork
25 Lower Abbey Street, Dublin 1.

© John B. Keane, 1979.

ISBN 0 85342 610 4

Music Arrangements: Eileen Barry.

To my friend

PAT KELLY

The Buds of Ballybunion was first produced at the White Memorial Theatre, Clonmel, on Friday 7 July 1978 with the following cast:

Mary O'Dea	Marie Twomey
Dolly O'Dea	Joey Cronin
Mr Moon	Charles Ginnane
The Boozer Mullane and other roles	James N. Healy
Tom Shaun Shea	Flor Dullea
Con Somers	Chris Sheehan
Molly Somers	Mairin Prendergast
Tessie Nix	Monica Murphy
Bessie Nix	Valerie Carroll
Mrs Bunce	Kay Healy
Mrs Black	Mary Foley
Father Bunce	Dan Donovan

Music by : Na Fili.

Play directed by Dan Donovan.

Overall Production by James N. Healy.

Stage Manager	Aidan O'Brien
Assistants	Julian Dillon and Dermot Hayes
Decor	Patrick Murray

Publicity : Donn McMullin and James Queally.

Sound	Tony Perrott
Photography	Paul O'Flynn

ACT ONE

Scene One

Young Dolly O'Dea and her mother Mary are seated on an ancient garden seat outside the O'Dea lodging house in Ballybunion.

Mary: Any time now and they'll be here.

Dolly: I'll look. *(She rises and goes towards the exit, peers into distance)* Not a sign that ever was.

Mary: Has Mr Moon got out of bed yet?

Dolly: There was a bump on the floor of his room a few minutes ago so he must be up.

Mary: If he doesn't appear soon he'll miss the arrival.

Dolly: Here he comes now. The man himself.
(Enter Moon from lodging house. He is an elderly little man wearing a bowler hat and an ancient navy blue suit, stiff collar and high boots.)

Moon: Any sign of them?

Mary: Any moment now I should think.

Moon: I always know that summer is officially over and autumn officially established as soon as the Buds arrive.

Dolly: Me too Mr Moon. Me too.
(She dances out into centre of stage and sings:)

THEY'RE BACK IN TOWN ONCE MORE
                    Words & Music: John B. Keane Arr. Eileen Barry.

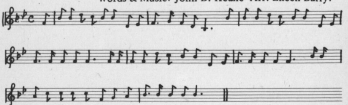

7

I know the summer's ended and the autumn's settled down
It's not because the corn is cut or nuts are turning brown.
It's not because the air's grown crisp or seaweed decks the shore
It's the Buds of Ballybunion. They've come back to town once more.

(Mr Moon and Mary join her and they walk back and forth singing the refrain:)

Oh they're back in town once more.
Oh they're back in town once more.
It's the Buds of Ballybunion and they're back in town once more.

Dolly:

I know the summer's ended and the young folk gone away.
The swallow's drifted south again. The barns are filled with hay.
But I'm only sure the summer's gone when I hear that old encore,
It's the Buds of Ballybunion. They've come back to town once more.

(All three sing refrain:)

Dolly:

So come all ye pleasant country folk who till the good red earth
We'll sing a sweet September song. We'll sing for all we're worth.
We'll sing it high and handsome and we'll stomp upon the floor,
For the Buds of Ballybunion have come back to town once more.

(All sing refrain and then repeat last verse together).
Moon: Dolly you're a tonic.

8

Dolly: You're another Mr Moon. You're another. I'll go and see if they're coming.

(Exit Dolly).

Moon: This must be the finest day we've had since June.

Mary: September is never without sunny days.

Moon: Better air too, crisper, cooler. It's like champagne this time of the year.

Mary: Oh they know the time to come alright. Make no mistake about that. Personally I wouldn't swap September for the three months of summer.

Moon: They should be here. Whatever's keeping them? The bus passed Ahafona Cross five minutes ago. I saw it from my window.

Mary: They'll have to unload their belongings. Then there's all that food. Here comes Dolly. They won't be far behind.

(Enter Dolly. She dances around the stage, singing and shouting).

Dolly: They're landed. They're landed. The Buds are landed. Open your doors Ballybunion. The Buds are back in town.

Moon: Any absentees?

Dolly: Not a one. All present and correct.

(Sings:)

The Buds of Ballybunion have arrived in town once more,

With carrots, kale and cabbages and turnips too galore.

With your buns and scones and pancakes, with your sugar, eggs and tay,

Oh you Buds of Ballybunion, you're as welcome as the May.

Moon: As the oldest Bud of all on behalf of all the Buds I thank you kindly.

(Enter the Boozer Mullane carrying suitcases. He wears an old cap, overcoat, turned down wellingtons. He deposits suitcases).

9

Boozer: (*Sings*)

In came the Ballybunion Buds their vittles for to ate,

'Twas hard-boiled eggs and griddle bread and lumps of hairy mate.

'Twas hard-boiled eggs for breakfast and 'twas soft-boiled eggs for tay,

You could hear the craturs clocking and they facing for the say.

(*Enter the Buds led by Tom Shaun Shea. Then come the Misses Nix, Tessie and Bessie. Then Con Somers and Molly Somers. Then The Widows, Mrs Bunce and Mrs Black. All carry bags and satchels of vegetables, bread, eggs and bacon. The Boozer relieves them and places all their belongings to one side. Each give him a few pence*).

Tom: Oh the air, the air. 'Twould bring a man from the dead.

Con: The air of Ballybunion would blow any blight anyway.

Mary: Leave your bags where they are now for the moment and we'll all go indoors to freshen up.

Tom: A noble idea Mary but we'll dance a step or two first to unravel the muscles after the journey and knock the rust off our bones. My father used always say that dancing was the only cure for pains. Give us a start there Mary. (*To others*) Come along now, take your partners for an old-time waltz.

(*Moon takes Dolly. The Widows and Nixes each other. Con takes Molly. Tom Shaun takes Mary. All waltz. After a circuit or two Mary and Tom come upstage*).

Mary: BALLYBUNION SONG *Words: John B. Keane Music: Anon.*

10

'Tis nice to see you all again this lovely autumn day,
To each and every one of you my heart says come to
    stay.
Come bathe in crystal waters were the green seas ebb
    and flow,
In dear old Ballybunion where the Shannon breezes
    blow.

Moon:
You ask me where I'd like to be when I am old and grey,
Where morning melts the green seas mists, where shoots
    the silver spray.
Where all the fields were green my love when we were
    young and gay,
Beyond in Ballybunion on a bright September day.
(All repeat this verse as they waltz).

Tom: Now all indoors for to freshen up. One... two...
three...
*(They dance into house to reel music. The Boozer
Mullane remains).*

Boozer: Are you wonderin' who that lot are or wonderin'
who I am myself? I'm only the Boozer Mullane. I don't
count. I'm only a bag carrier, a message boy, a bum,
always on the make for booze but those now, that lot
that went in there, they're different. They are the Buds
of Ballybunion. They are here as always for the fall-of-
the year holiday. Bud, of course, is an abbreviation of
the Gaelic word, *Bodaire,* meaning a sort of rough country
person. This is their yearly break before the snows of
winter whiten the hills. They bring with them their own
eggs, bacon, bread, butter, jam, cabbage, spuds etcetera.
They pay for the lodgings and Mary O'Dea does the
cooking. They are, alas, the very last of their kind. Here
they come now for the evening stroll. I'll draw aside and
introduce them.
(Enter Con and Molly Somers, linking arms).

11

Molly: What time is it Con dear?

Con: Wanting but two minutes my love for nine of the clock.

Molly: Shall we turn dearest?

Con: Not yet my sweet. We'll do another round of the houses and then we'll turn.

Molly: Whatever you say Con darling, whatever you say.
(Exit Con and Molly Somers).

Boozer: There goes Con Somers and Molly his wife,
A couple who never knew anguish or strife.
The fossil approaching is old Mr Moon,
He's well over eighty but jaunty as June.
(Enter Mr Moon, pondering weighty issues to himself.)

Boozer: And now comes a sunbeam all cheerful and gay,
'Tis that bright little angel sweet Dolly O'Dea.
(Enter Dolly bearing a basket).

Dolly: Hello Mr Moon.

Moon: (Waking from his trance) Who? Who? Who is it? Ah Dolly my dear 'tis yourself that adorns the heel of the evening.

Dolly: How's life Mr Moon?

Moon: Life Dolly? What is life?

Dolly: What is life Mr Moon? If anyone knows you do.

Moon: Life is just a seed Dolly. You and I are the crops. Of course you'd be more of a flower I'm thinking. You are the ripening bud Dolly and I am the fading leaf. We come Dolly and we go.

Dolly: We come and we go Mr Moon.

Moon: We come and we go Dolly. We do indeed. We come and we go so we do but the seed remains. Therefore, we ourselves remain, not entirely but in part which is better of course than if nothing at all remained.

Dolly: Oh of course Mr Moon. Of course, of course, of course.
(Exit Dolly to house).

Moon: Of course, of course. What was I talking about. I'd

12

better ask Dolly. Dolly? Dolly? But who's Dolly? That's
a good one. Who is Dolly? That's a good one. Dolly?
Dolly?
(Exit pondering).

Boozer: The next for inspection is poor Tom Shaun Shea,
    A regular hayseed and clown in his way,
    You'll hear him extolling to the spinsters Miss Nix,
    All about his late father and that bold hero's tricks.
(Enter Tom Shaun and the Misses Nix).

Tom: My father was an almighty man. He'd never do anything by half. Catch him buying a single suit of clothes.
You'd catch a weasel asleep first. He'd weigh a likely
boult of cloth for a long while in his two hands, big
hairy hands the size of frying pans.

Tessie: (Aside) Hairy? Ugh?

Tom: When he had the cloth weighed he'd let it dribble
over his fingers on to the floor. This was to feel for flaws.
Then the two eyes would close by him while he felt the
texture of the material between his thumb and fingers.
He'd stand there like he'd be in a trance. Boult after
boult he'd go through till he'd find a one that matched
all his expectations.

Bessie: Would he buy the whole boult?

Tessie: Of course he would. He'd never do anything by half.

Tom: Oh that was my father God be good to him, the
whole boult, nothing else.

Bessie: A far-seeing man, a thoughtful man, not like the
men of today.

Tom: No indeed. Not like the men of today at all.
(Exit Tom and Bessie).

Tessie: Men of today my eye! Who'd want the men of
today? Horrid hairy devils.
(Exit Tessie).

Boozer: Now here come a dour pair, Mrs Black and Mrs
    Bunce,
    Both widowed and ancient I'll tell you at once.

13

They both live, alas, with their daughters-in-law,
In constant confusion and permanent war.

Mrs Black: And how is your dear and darling daughter-in-law these days Mrs Bunce?

Mrs Bunce: The same as always. There is no chance from that quarter God help us. And how is your own daughter-in-law? *(Offers her a pinch of snuff).*

Mrs Black: (Accepts snuff and sniffs it) There is no change from that quarter either I assure you. It galls me day in day out to see the home I built so lovingly over a lifetime in the hands of a stranger.

Mrs Bunce: Without a voice in the proceedings.

Mrs Black: With no say at all God pity us.

Mrs Bunce: Often confined like a common criminal to my room.

Mrs Black: Daring not to move hither or thither. I have often longed for death Mrs Bunce.

Mrs Bunce: And how often do I pray for a speedy release from the monster that turned my own son against me. *(Exit both).*

Boozer: Any minute now they'll all be back and the nightly ritual will begin. The men will retire to the pub to lubricate their tonsils and the women will sit in the kitchen going over the gossip of the year. Then the men will return after an hour or two with any fresh news which might happen to be going the rounds. Here they come now, dead on course and dead on time. *(Enter Tom Shaun with the Misses Nix).*

Tom: My father now when he would be getting his hair cut would forego the normal system of trimming. Let the bone be your guide he'd tell the barber and sure enough when the job was done you'd stand a better chance of finding hair on a beach ball. Bald as an apple he'd be. *(Enter Con and Molly).*

Molly: You won't be long love.

Con: I won't be long dearest.

14

Molly: I'll miss you.

Con: And I'll miss you my darling.

Molly: (Going indoors with the Misses Nix) 'Bye for awhile dearest one.

Con: 'Bye love.

(Enter Moon. Followed by the Widows. He joins Tom and Con).

Mrs Black: Off to the pub I suppose.

Mrs Bunce: (As they exit to house) Drink, drink, drink. That's all the men think of.

(Exit both).

Moon: Oh we think of more than that my lassie. There's more to us than beer and skittles. Eh lads?

Tom: Ahem . . . Yes, yes of course. Shall we wet our whistles boys?

Moon: By all means.

Con: What a fierce fine evening it is.

Tom: Ah yes you may say so. There's a mighty red sun sinking out there in the ocean and there's a red horizon to match it. A red horizon my father used always say was the very thing for fine days, fine dry days, sunny and clear. Let us be going then. *(To Boozer)* Come on Boozer. You don't want to be left behind do you?

(Exit Tom Shaun, Oul' Moon and Con).

Boozer: To be a successful bum you need brains, education and a cheerful disposition. It has taken me years to get where I am today. It wasn't easy remaining idle while everybody else was working but I persevered. I ignored the jibes and the abuse because I knew that one day I'd take my rightful place in the world as a fully qualified, fully-fledged bum.

(Exit Boozer).

CURTAIN
for end of Scene 1, Act 1

ACT ONE

Scene Two

Women talk in kitchen before return of men. They sit around the old herald range talking).

Mary: How did the turkeys go with you this year, Miss Bessie?

Bessie: Often better, Mary dear. The eggs were slow to hatch and when they did the fox swept five. Another was carried in a brown flood and two died after putting out the red heads. Five more wandered and came back no more.

Tessie: All we have for the Christmas market is a dozen birds.

Mrs Black: Have ye got good cocks around your way, Miss Bessie?

Tessie: We have no cocks of our own.

Mrs Black: But haven't your neighbours got cocks?

Bessie: Our nearest neighbour has a fine cock.

Tessie: He never failed us yet. He's as reliable a cock as you'd find.

Molly: Aren't ye lucky. I have to travel miles for a cock.

Mrs Black: And pray Molly Somers, is he a station cock?

Molly: Well he's not a station cock Mrs Black, but he services every bird for miles around. I never heard a hen ask was he station or common.

Mrs Black: I wouldn't let my bird near a common cock. It's a station cock for me no matter what.

Molly: I imagine a cock you know is better than a cock you don't know.

Mrs Bunce: If you have none of your own there's a lot to be said for a neighbour's cock.

Mrs Black: You're all entitled to your opinion, but a

16

station cock is certified by the poultry instructress. She ought to know, she's handling cocks every day.

Mrs Bunce: It's all luck. You could be lucky with a bad cock or a good cock could break your heart.

Molly: You can't really depend on any cock.

Mrs Bunce: Oh no cock is to be trusted.

Mrs Black: Well now, my advice to you Miss Bessie and Miss Tessie is to have no more to do with local cocks. You just can't trust a local cock. When your hen starts to lie and passes her first egg, bundle her into a bag and land her to the nearest station cock. Make sure that no hen was serviced before you. Make sure you get the first dart of the day and you'll never touch an ordinary cock again.

Mary: Here come the men. Say no more about cocks now. *(Enter men).*

Tom: And will you tell me now what happened to the foxy-haired boy from Newmarket that used to keep the pony stallion?

Con: Ah, God be good to him he's dead this year past the poor man. The widow sold the place. She's living in the town now. And tell me — your man with the one eye and the bald head that used to play for Shanballymore? Is he here or there?

Moon: Oh, faith he's here the whole time. He has a public house now in Buttevant and four sons from what I'm told.

Con: Did any of the boys take up the hurley?

Moon: God knows, I hear they're pucking. The eldest boy, they say, will wear the county jersey.

Tom: Well I declare to God but isn't breeding a holy terror the way it breaks out.

Moon: Man dear, there's breeding in turnips.

Tom: Breeding in turnips there is to be sure. And how're the ladies? *(Cross to ladies)* Hard at it girls.

Molly: You came to no harm, Con?

Tom: Divil a harm woman, only a belly full of lukewarm porter. My father often said —

Mary: (Hastily) What about a touch of that poem, Tom Shaun, that you gave us that night last year?

Tom: I'll tell ye no poem but I'll tell ye a new joke I heard in the pub down below. You see, there was this fellow —

Con: We met this fellow in the pub that told us he had the longest kick of a football ever recorded.
(Others confirm).

Con: This fellow hails from the village of Ballyduff and in the year 1920 he placed a ball outside his back door on a triopal of grass with a view to breaking the world record. He went back forty yards from the ball and ran at it like a bull to a heifer. He hit it a flake and it soared into the sky where it burst. The cover of that ball landed in the Isle of Man.

Molly: And the bladder?

Con: The bladder landed in Boonees Airees outside the hall door of a whorehouse.

Mrs Bunce: Oh shame, shame, shame.

Tom: Well now it's my noble call and I call on Con Somers to give us the song he gave us below in the pub.
(Faint applause).

Molly: Con you weren't singing in a public house?

Tom: Why wouldn't he be?

Tessie: I never heard Con singing.

Tom: Fakes you're going to hear him now.

Molly: It's not dirty is it Con?

Con: Yirra not at all love — it's about an old farm labourer beyond Listowel.

Tom: Off you go Con.
(Con stands up and sings. All clap hands gently as he sings. Men might dance a step or two).

THE BRADYS OF KILLANNE

Words & Music: Anon Arr. Eileen Barry

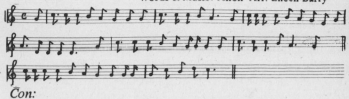

Con:

When I went down to the iron bridge the place they call
    the strand,
'Twas there I hired for seven long years with the Bradys
    of Killanne,
The morning that I hired with them 'twas plainly I could
    see,
They promised me eggs and bacon and they then shook
    hands with me,
Saying you're welcome to my house Johnny O, you're
    with a decent man.

When I woke up next mornin' I heard a terrible row,
'Twas the getting up of Brady or the gruntin' of a sow,
'Hurry up there with the water, make a sup of salts for
    Nan',
'Twas ever and all the same old call at Bradys of Killanne.

When I went into bed at night, 'twas loudly I did bawl,
The fleas they made a strong attack, my kidneys for to
    haul.
With scratching and with tearing, my skin grew like a tan,
I roared and bawled and kicked the walls at the Bradys
    of Killanne.

When I worked out on the farm my hair grew like a wig,
My coat it got too small for me, my trousers got too big.
I'm sending for Mickeen Hennessy, he'll be on now soon
    with the van,

To handcart me to the County Home from the Bradys of
Killanne.

Tom: Well done, well done.

Con: That's all I remember of it.

Mrs Bunce: That much will do fine.

Mrs Black: 'Tis enough.

Tom: My father knew so many songs by heart you might
say he was a walking song-book. I declare to God he
could sing all night. This woman that had a travelling
show asked him to name his own fee. I remember another
occasion. . .

Mary: (Hastily) And what about the dance? You'd hardly
go to bed your first night in the house without 'Patsy
Healy'. Will you organise them there Mr Moon.

*(But Moon is off in a world of his own. Music of Patsy
Healy is heard).*

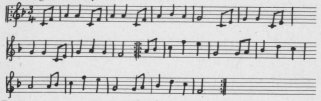

Dolly: Come on Mr Moon, you and me together.

Moon: I will. I will. I will to be sure. Dolly will dance with
me, and Mary O'Dea with Tom Shaun; and the Nix girls
together and the Widows together and of course Con and
Molly.

*(The Nixes pair off. The Widows pair off. The others
pair off and they complete the dance. As they come to
the end the clock strikes twelve and the dance suddenly
stops. All produce Rosary beads and all kneel except
Moon. Mary leads off and the others answer. After three
Hail Marys the lights begin to fade).*

CURTAIN

for end of Scene 2, Act 1.

ACT ONE

Scene Three

Kitchen, the following morning. Mary busy at table. Enter Dolly.

Mary: Dolly! Time to get the breakfast Dolly. Are they all in from Mass?

Dolly: Not yet. Mr Moon never got up for it.

Mary: That's nothing new.

Dolly: He has the affairs of the world settled talking to himself all the morning.

Mary: He's old Dolly. He dotes a little.

Dolly: He still has the wandering eye. I often see him ogling girls down on the strand.

Mary: There's no harm in that.

(Dolly assists with shifting and laying of table).

Dolly: I was thinking last night mother before I fell asleep.

Mary: Out with it Dolly. What were you thinking?

Dolly: I could get a job.

Mary: We've been through all this before Dolly. You know my views on the matter.

Dolly: But mother I'm fifteen. I don't want to go on being a burden to you.

Mary: I assure you you're no burden Dolly. You'll finish school and then you'll go to the university.

Dolly: But the money mother. Where's the money to come from?

Mary: We've managed up to this haven't we?

Dolly: But it's all work and worry for you across the summer. You never take a break.

Mary: I don't need a break.

Dolly: Every penny you earn goes on me.

Mary: And that is as it should be. You're all I have Dolly and I want the best for you. Please God you'll marry some day and have a family. God forbid that anything should happen your husband but if it ever does you'll have your profession to fall back on, not like me.

Dolly: I don't think I'm good enough to get through university.

Mary: When the times comes you'll be good enough. Now pretty up that table.

(Enter Mr Moon in waistcoat and pants).

Dolly: How's life Mr Moon?

Moon: Life Dolly? Life? Why should I care about life?

Dolly: Why shouldn't you?

Moon: Because Dolly the life which I have loved so well will shortly abandon me callously and mercilessly to suit it own cycle. So why should I care? I wouldn't give you a solitary cockle-shell for what's left of my life.

Dolly: You mustn't say that Mr Moon.

Moon: We come and we go Dolly. Remember.

Dolly: We come and we go Mr Moon.

Moon: Would you be so kind Dolly as to go to my room and fetch me one speckled hen egg and one blue duck egg from the suitcase under the bed?

Dolly: Yes Mr Moon.

Moon: Then would you go to the other suitcase, Dolly dear, and fetch my small pot of red jam and my little jar of butter.

Dolly: One speckled hen egg Mr Moon and one blue duck egg, your small pot of red jam and your little jar of butter.

(Exit Dolly repeating Moon's request. Moon coughs a little).

Mary: Are you alright Mr Moon?

Moon: I'm fine Mary. Fine as a chap of my age could hope to be.

Mary: Which is Mr Moon?

22

Moon: Which is two along of eighty.

Mary: Two along of eighty. 'Tis few sees the four score Mr Moon.

(Enter Tom Shaun and the Misses Nix from Mass).

Tom: My father of course would never be fobbed off with a hen egg or a duck egg.

Bessie: What sort of egg would he eat then?

Tom: He would eat a goose egg Miss Bessie. Nothing less than a goose egg would do him.

Tessie: Would he eat it all?

Bessie: Of course he would.

Tom: Every last morsel Miss Tessie. Not as much as a toothful to be seen in the shell when he finished. Of course he was a superior type of man in every possible way. He'd never countenance cursing under his roof and never once did I hear a swear-word fall from his mouth, under no circumstance would he ever bore a man. I'm like him in that respect.

(Exit all three to rooms).

Moon: He'll never be any good the poor fellow. He's only the shadow of his father.

Mary: But he's such a kind man. Such a gentleman.

Moon: Aye kind but a pure rake, poor chap.

(Enter Widows).

Mrs Bunce: Good morning Mary.

Mary: Hello ladies.

Mrs Bunce: (To Moon) Morning.

Mrs Black: (As if she doesn't think so) Good morning.

Mrs Bunce: I'm killed from consomnia.

Moon: What in God's name is that?

Mrs Black: It means she can't sleep and no wonder with the life she has. 'Tis a wonder we're alive at all the two of us the persecution we get.

(Exit both to rooms).

Moon: Always hinting about the daughters-in-law. Are they really as bad as they're painted or are those two the

THE BUDS OF BALLYBUNION

authors of their own misfortune?

Mary: By all accounts Mr Moon there's no hornet the equal of young Mrs Bunce and there's no wasp with the sting of young Mrs Black.

Moon: Why don't they leave? Young folk must be left to themselves. I know I'd leave.

Mary: Leave? At seventy-five leave your own hearth? Anyway where is there to go unless you want them in the county home or a room in town where everyone is a black stranger. Is this to be their thanks at the end of their days?

(Enter Con and Molly. They are absorbed and don't notice others. They are holding hands).

Molly: And pray what time is it now Con my dear?

Con: The time now my love is six and half minutes past nine of the clock and anyone that says it's later or earlier is not far short of being a fool.

Molly: The clock on the wall there says it's ten minutes past.

Con: Then the clock on the wall is wrong for this Swiss watch of mine has to gain or lose a second from the day it was put together in the village of Oomplestonk in Switzerland in the year of Our Lord eighteen hundred and ninety seven.

Molly: How much time is left to us Con?

Con: To us my love?

Molly: You and I and no other Con. Con my dearest one, my sweet Con the bon-bon.

Con: We have left thirteen days and twelve hours my darling Molly.

Molly: How quickly the time has passed.

Con: That's the way with time my love, fast when you want it slow and slow when you want it fast. Still we have thirteen days remaining. The weather is dry. The wind is from a good quarter and we're together.

Molly: I'm looking forward to tonight.

Con: Not half as much as I dear Molly Dolly so jolly. Not half as much as I.

(They kiss and exit).

Moon: They live for the holiday here. They'll spend the months in-between counting the days. It's the only diversion they have God help us. You might say the thought of it keeps them alive.

(Enter Dolly. She places Moon's requests in front of him).

Mary: Yes . . . One must cling to something.

Moon: I don't know. When a person's quota is filled I think they should settle for that and not be teasing out extra time. Me now . . . I've had my share. Let the end come when it will. You won't find me asking for more.

Mary: That's a great way to be Mr Moon. 'Tis fine to be so resigned.

(Enter all the others. They line up to range where Dolly receives their requests).

Dolly: Boiled soft isn't it Mrs Bunce?

Mrs Bunce: Yes Dolly. Boiled soft.

Dolly: One white hen egg. Boiled soft. *(Writes on egg with pencil)* S. for soft. B. for Bunce.

(Next in line is Mrs Black).

Mrs Black: Same for me. Boiled soft.

Dolly: One dark brown hen egg. Bl. for Mrs Black. S. for soft.

Con: Please acknowledge hen eggs three. One for her and two for me and boiled as soft as they can be.

Dolly: S. for Somers. S. for soft.

Tessie: We don't want them hard.

Dolly: I know Miss Tessie. You don't want them hard and you don't want them soft. You want them in-between.

Bessie: In-between exactly.

Dolly: M. for Misses, N. for Nix. B. for between.

Moon: (From table) You know me Dolly.

Dolly: Medium rare for Mr Moon. M.M. M.R.

25

Tom Shaun: Two duck eggs Dolly. One pale blue, the other sea green, to be given such a boiling as never was seen.

Dolly: Hard for Tom Shaun.

Tom Shaun: Hard as the rocks of Bawn, Dolly. Hard as the hobs of hell. Hard as two cannon. . . .

Moon: Balls!

Tom Shaun: If you say so, Mr Moon.

Dolly: T.S. for Tom Shaun. H. for hard.

Mary: Time to wet the tea.

Con: (Holding up watch) Us is done now Dolly. You can be taking them up.

Dolly: Right away Mr Somers. Here they are.

Mrs Bunce: Who will say grace this morning?

Moon: Oh Tom Shaun of course. His voice is the clearest of all.

Dolly: And the dearest of all.
  (Tom Shaun rises. All rise).

Tom: Bless us O Lord and these Thy gifts which of Thy bounty we are about to receive through Christ our Lord. Amen.

All: Amen.
  (They start to dine).

Tom: What will the weather do Mr Moon? You're the expert.

Moon: I must say it's as fine an autumn as ever came. I'm of the opinion it will hold. My bones are my advisers in this respect and they tell me in their own quiet way that the outlook is good.

Dolly: One soft hen egg for Mrs Bunce and one soft hen egg for Mrs Black.

  (She delivers them to table).

Tom: And how long would you be coming here now Mr Moon?

Moon: A long, long time indeed. Let me see now. Man and

boy I reckon it would be nigh on seventy years. The old folk were young folk when I started coming the Lord be good to them all.

Dolly: N. for the Miss Nixes, boiled in-between.
(She delivers).

Tessie: You must have seen many changes over the years Mr Moon.

Moon: Not so many. The diet is much the same as always. People much the same. Weather much the same. We come and we go. Then one day the whole thing is over. Just like that. The whole thing is over.

Dolly: M.M. for Mr Moon, medium rare. One speckled hen egg and one blue duck egg.

Moon: Thank you Dolly.

Tessie: And pray Tom Shaun how long have you been coming here?

Tom: A goodly while Miss Tessie. I came here first with my father when I was ten. I too remember the old folk. My father would kill a pig a month before. That pig would then be salted and four of the finest, streakiest flitches together with the hams and gams would be transported here along with a hundred of eggs, a butt of spuds and a sack of flour for pancakes. The rest of the victuals would be bought local, carrots, parsnips, peas and beans, beefsteak and mutton rashers.

Dolly: Mutton rashers, what are they?

Moon: Chops my dear Dolly, simply chops.

Bessie: But who would eat it all? The bacon, the hams, the flour, the potatoes, the vegetables?

Tom: Him and me. My sainted father and my humble self.

Bessie: And nobody else?

Tom: Him and me and no more.

Bessie: And where was your mother?

Tom: She died the day I was born Miss Bessie. That left me and him thrown together all the time. When he left here at the end of the month there would be no flour left, there would be no egg and not as much bacon as would grease the hinges of Mrs Bunce's snuff box.

Dolly: Tom Shaun. One pale blue, the other sea green and given such a boiling as never was seen.

Tom: Thank you Dolly.

Bessie: But you didn't say how long you were coming?

Tom: My father it was that showed me how to take the cap from my first egg. Tap gently round and round, round and round, as if 'twas your own head you were tapping. Then firmly thrust the spoon through the fractured area thus removing the cap with no shell on your lap, none on your table and none . . . *(Egg lands on his lap. All laugh).*

Dolly: None on your hands?

Tom: Precisely. *(Dries his hands on table cloth)* You were saying Miss Bessie?

Bessie: I was asking how long have you been coming to Ballybunion?

Tom: I was ten when I came first and I am presently facing my fiftieth year.

Bessie: Then you would be coming here for forty years.

Tom: Not all told. You see when my father died I took to the bottle in earnest. I played the rake for five years, nearly drank myself out of my farm.

Bessie: Then you are thirty-five years coming.

Tom: Mathematically speaking that would be correct but in human terms there were years when I was here yet I wasn't here at all. I lived in a drunken daze. There was never an hour when there wasn't a smell of whiskey off me. But for Mary O'Dea here I'd be growing daisies this living minute. She kept the bite and sup to me and my bed was always here, clean, soft and warm. I was able to return to my farm with some semblance of health the last day of September.

Bessie: You mean you've reformed?

Moon: What he means is that he has learned how to take

his drink in a civilised manner and has discovered there is more to life than the inside of a public house.

Tom: Hear, hear. Hear, hear. I used to be a walking brewery although I daresay I staggered more than I walked.

Mrs Black: When did you see the light?

Tom: I remember the day exactly. I was sitting with a glass of whiskey in my hand in the Atlantic Bar in the snug where no one could see me. These two fellows came into the public bar and called for two glasses of stout. Then one said to the other: 'Have you seen Tom Shaun Shea lately?' and the other: 'Who wants to see that gander?' 'Now, now,' said the other, 'aren't you being hard on ganders?' 'I would say he's more of a dunkey.' 'But isn't a dunkey a useful chap?' said the second fellow. I gathered I wasn't fit company for man or beast. I was a drunkard, a messer and an all-round general nuisance. When I left that snug that morning my mind was made up. No more malt whiskey for me. No more long boozes. Drink yes and in plenty but never again would I be so suffocated with alcohol that I was a danger to myself and my own kind.

Tessie: Men do what they like.

Moon: The drinking laws are the same for both sexes.

Tessie: I've never crossed the door of a public house.

Bessie: Neither have I.

Moon: There's no one to stop you.

Tessie: Yes there is.

Moon: Pray what?

Tessie: Men that's what. There's nothing but men. Big, rough, hairy men mostly drunk and mostly dirty, present company excepted, of course.

Moon: Of course, of course, present company accepted.

(Knock at door. An elderly gentleman [outsider] is seen outside. Morning coat, bowler hat and briefcase).

Mary: I wonder who that is? Dolly, will you see to the door?

29

(Dolly does so).

Dolly: Ma'am, it's Mr Maloney, the Solicitor from Listowel.

Mary: Oh goodness and look at the cut of the place. Folks, would you ever mind taking the table into the other room if you haven't finished breakfast. *(They do this with a good deal of assenting talk)* Come in, Mr Maloney, excuse the condition of the place.

Maloney: (Somewhat prissy) Oh, that's alright Mary. I've been in worse in my time.

Mary: Will you sit down?

Maloney: Yes, I'll sit and I think you'd better do so too, for while I wish I was bringing better news as often in my profession I am not. Now you've lived in this house all your life, have you not?

Mary: Yes Mr Maloney.

Maloney: And your mother before you?

Mary: Yes indeed.

Maloney: I knew the poor woman well, God rest her. Now five years ago you raised a mortgage on the premises with a Mrs Isolde Wantmore of the Ready to Lend Credit Company?

Mary: What else could I do at the time. The place was falling down.

Maloney: Yes, I know the circumstances although I might have advised you differently had I been given the opportunity. Now I have to advise you dear Mary that unless the full amount of the loan and the accumulated interest is paid at once Mrs Wantmore intends to foreclose on the mortgage or so I am informed by her solicitors, Totcher, Botcher and Gotcher.

Mary: Oh dear.

Maloney: Oh dear hardly covers it. You made no attempt to repay the loan Mary.

Mary: I tried but I couldn't make ends meet. I just don't have the money Mr Maloney.

Maloney: Then it seems you'll have to leave. I could help

find a position for you.

Mary: I can never leave here Mr Maloney.

Maloney: Why not?

Mary: Because my husband is buried here.

Maloney: Your husband is dead with years.

Mary: There are too many memories.

Maloney: You're alive Mary. Still young. Memories belong to the past.

Mary: I can't leave him.

Maloney: He doesn't exist anymore. There's just a grave and a headstone. You can leave those.

Mary: I can't.

Maloney: But he was a waster. He never did a stroke of work in his life. I wouldn't presume to speak to you like this but I have a responsibility towards you. I am also an old family friend. Your late husband is the real cause of your present plight.

Mary: I loved him.

Maloney: He didn't love you.

Mary: In his own way he did.

Maloney: He loved himself.

Mary: No. He loved me.

Maloney: If he loved you he wouldn't have allowed you to support him. He'd have provided for you, for Dolly. That's what love is — cherish his memory by all means but get out of here. You'll get a job. You're a good cook.

Mary: I can't leave him.

Maloney: He left you didn't he? When you were warm and tender and brimming with love he left you for the tavern and for heaven knows what.

Mary: It isn't true.

Maloney: For God's sake when are you going to be honest with yourself? He drank every penny you ever earned. He left you up to your ears in debt. How many times in the grey of the morning did he tumble into your bed reeking with the perfume of holiday girls? When you needed him most he was never there.

Mary: Why do you torment me?

Maloney: You know me Mary and I know you since you were two years old. You know I'd help in any way I can but you'd better make up your mind that your days in this house are numbered.

Mary: But what am I going to do about the Buds?

Maloney: You've spent all your life thinking about other people; time now that you started thinking about yourself. Don't forget — call on me if there is anything I can do.

(Exit Maloney).

Mary: (Sings:)

Goodbye to Ballybunion where the green seas ebb and flow

Goodbye to every lofty cliff and golden sands below.

Farewell, farewell, my own true love, the time has come to go,

Goodbye to Ballybunion, where the Shannon waters flow.

(She goes off sadly as Maloney who has returned to stand outside and listen starts to close the door).

Maloney: Now if I was the marrying kind — which I'm not — there's a woman I would confront with my litany of loneliness. But as that's not possible I'd better settle for the next best thing — time for a small one or two before I cycle back to Listowel.

(He trots off quickly).

CURTAIN

for end of Scene 3, Act 1.

ACT ONE

Scene Four

Enter Tessie and Bessie in period bathing costumes and caps. They cautiously emerge from lodgings.

Tessie: I dread the thought of going home.

Bessie: Which home?

Tessie: Please Bessie. That was never a home. I never even slept there.

Bessie: Legally it is your home. He was and is your husband.

Tessie: Legally. Well legally or otherwise the marriage was never consummated.

Bessie: How long has it been now?

Tessie: Eight years.

Bessie: Do you wish to talk about it?

Tessie: I never want to talk about that — never! Oh the men are coming. Let's move off quickly to the caves.
(Enter Tom and Moon in bare feet with trousers rolled up to the knees. They carry shoes in hands).

Tom: There is no place like the sea when the day is fine.

Moon: I intend today to paddle till the legs give out on me.

Tom: Me too.

Moon: And can you not swim, a young chap like you should take the plunge.

Tom: I swim the same as a stone. My father now. Ah by God there was a swimmer. Of course he had arms like iron. Like a whale in the water he was, snorting and diving and spitting salt water over his mighty shoulders. What a figure of a man he was. You couldn't get me into the water but you couldn't get him out of it.

Moon: I recall him well. A powerful swimmer to be sure.

33

(Both move off. Enter Con and Molly from house. Molly wears coat over bathing togs).

Con: I suppose you'll take yourself to the caves for a wash with the rest of the girls?

Molly: 'Tis a day for it my love.

Con: I'll paddle by the shore but my heart will be with you.

Molly: I'll come if you like.

Con: No. Have your bathe. As you say 'tis a day for it. I'll see you God willing on the castle green at five of the clock. The village clock will strike the five hours and you'll know it's time to meet me.

Molly: And then?

Con: And then my love we'll sojourn to the handiest pub where we will drink a glass of creamy stout it being the very thing to put a fine edge on a body's appetite. *(Molly goes to cave. Con joins men. Enter Widows from house, coats over ancient bathing costumes. Fr Bunce passes totally absorbed with the reading of his Office).*

Mrs Bunce: I never saw time to go so quickly.

Mrs Black: That's because of what's facing us when we leave. Come let's put the thought of those two viragos out of our minds for the day.

Mrs Bunce: You go on. I'll follow. I'd like a word with my son.

Mrs Black: I'll be in the cave with the others.

Mrs Bunce: It's time we had a talk son.

Fr Bunce: Alright mother. We'll have a talk.

Mrs Bunce: I missed you this morning — at Mass.

Fr Bunce: I know. I slept out. I said a later Mass.

Mrs Bunce: You feeling alright?

Fr Bunce: I'll survive. There was a game of poker last night. We played till three in the morning and of course drank till the same hour. I have a terrible head today.

Mrs Bunce: You shouldn't drink so much.

Fr Bunce: I don't except on holidays. You have something

on your mind?

Mrs Bunce: It can wait if you don't feel well.

Fr Bunce: No it can't. My head would never be so bad that I couldn't hear out my own mother.

Mrs Bunce: I can't stay with my daughter-in-law any longer.

Fr Bunce: Mother we went into this before. You have no alternative.

Mrs Bunce: It's hell. She treats me like dirt.

Fr Bunce: Ignore her.

Mrs Bunce: How can I ignore her when we live in the same house, eat in the same kitchen, wash in the same sink?

Fr Bunce: Pretend she isn't there. Find refuge in prayer. Offer it up to God and you'll be the stronger and the happier for it.

Mrs Bunce: What sort of talk is that? I want help, not penance. I'm old and tired. I need comfort and nourishment and you tell me pray. I've been praying all my life and this is what I wind up with, a cold room, a corner out of the way, unwanted while they wait for me to die. I'm a hindrance in their living, an obstruction is what I am. You must take me out of there.

Fr Bunce: Me?

Mrs Bunce: You. Who else? You're my son.

Fr Bunce: But I have nowhere to put you. I know it's a terrible thing to say but you're not my responsibility, not any more.

Mrs Bunce: Then who's responsibility am I?

Fr Bunce: Your married son's. It's all in the Will. Wasn't I a witness. You were present and you were agreeable. You signed willingly, in my presence you signed.

Mrs Bunce: I didn't know what I was doing but Lord help me I know now.

Fr Bunce: Now mother don't take on. Each of us has a cross.

Mrs Bunce: What cross have you in God's name?

Fr Bunce: *(Points to his Roman collar)* This is my cross. I said goodbye to people, goodbye to love, goodbye to family the day I erected this barrier under my chin.

Mrs Bunce: You can't be serious.

Fr Bunce: Am I denied the right to be serious too. This collar may be white and stainless but underneath there's a heart with blood as red and as rich as any and you say I have no cross. You don't know what agony is, what torment means, what isolation can do to a man.

Mrs Bunce: What is to become of me?

Fr Bunce: You?

Mrs Bunce: Me. Your mother.

Fr Bunce: What can I do mother?

Mrs Bunce: But I have nobody.

Fr Bunce: You have God.

Mrs Bunce: Where is God when I need him?

Fr Bunce: Everywhere. God is everywhere.

Mrs Bunce: But you're my son. You must help me.

Fr Bunce: I know I'm your son but first and foremost and irrevocably I am a priest. Whatever little is left after that is your son. *(He returns to reading of Office).*

Mrs Bunce: So I'm to expect help from nowhere — pious platitudes and nothing more.

(She goes off to cave. He snaps Breviary shut).

CURTAIN
for end of Scene 4, Act 1.

ACT ONE

Scene Five

The pool near the caves. Tom, Moon and Con.

Con: I hear the women coming. They'll want this place to themselves.

Moon: So they will. So they will. Let's ramble off then. *(He dips toe in pool)* By the hokey 'tis cold.

Con: Do you expect it to be hot with the summer gone these past two months. *(Con dips toe in pool)* Oh by God you're right, it's cold, a man could get pneumonia out of this.

Tom: Aye and we've had frost at night. *(He dips toe)* Ho-ho, ho-ho. Someone's put ice in it. *(He dances around).*

Moon: Let's move. Here they come.

Con: Righto, let's go.

(Exit all three. Enter the women, all in togs).

Molly: *(Calls)* Are you looking for me Con love? Yoohoo, Con, yoohoo.

Bessie: There's no one here.

Molly: I thought I heard his voice.

Tessie: I hope they're not spying on us. *(Covers herself up).*

Mrs Black: A lot they'd see at our age.

Molly: Con would never do that.

Tessie: Never trust men I say.

(The Boozer Mullane hovers in background).

Mrs Black: Oh the merciful relief of a loosened corset.

Mrs Bunce: There's no freedom so sweet as the freedom of a belly released. *(Scatches her belly appreciatively).*

Boozer: *(Aside)* I suppose I should tell you that this is an annual ritual when the women of the party ceremonious-

ly wash themselves in the rock pool under the old castle
— not realising that I have a peep-hole up on the cliffs
from which I can see all or nearly all. Someday if I have
enough porter drank I'll take a running jump into the
middle of them.

Bessie: It's freezing.

Tessie: I never remember it to be so cold.

Mrs Black: The old people used to say there's no good in it
unless it has a sting. Oh! Oh!

Molly: My mother, God be good to her, used to say that
warm sea water was a mass of germs but that there was
every kind of a cure in it when it made you shiver. Oh!
Oh!

Bessie: It's making me shiver alright.

Tessie: Bessie control yourself.

Boozer: (Aside from hiding place) You see how the
occasion makes young women of old. Shortly now they
will immerse the lower parts of their bodies in the tidal
pool. This calls for courage and perseverance for please
to remember the bitterly cold salt water will suddenly
be spattered and splashed upon the most private, most
sensitive and most warm part, according to medical
evidence, of the female body, a sacred part which has
not seen the light of day shall we say since this time last
year and very often, God preserve their modesty, never
seen the light of day at all. Behold now the breaking of
the ice.

Bessie: Come on now who sits first? Mrs Bunce you're the
one.

Mrs Bunce: Oh no! I'm too old. Mrs Black is the very lady
for the job.

Mrs Black: My heart wouldn't stand it.

Bessie: I know what we'll do. We'll draw lots. All come
around now and stand without moving. Eenie, meenie,
minie mo. Catch an eejit by the toe. If he screeches let him
go. Eenie, meenie, minie, mo. You're the one Mrs Somers.

Let's get her girls.

(They seize Molly and slowly dip her backside into water. As soon as she touches it she erupts with a terrifying screech. They dip her again and again but the screeches become toned down until at last with a loud sigh she allows herself to be seated in the water.

Screams and sighs. They splash themselves and each other with obvious delight).

Tessie: 'Tis grand when you get used to it.

Bessie: Pass the soap and stop the chatter.

Molly: A song would be lovely now.

Bessie: All together so.

(They dance out of pool and around stage).

All:

Goodbye to Ballybunion where the green seas ebb and
    flow,

Goodbye to every lofty cliff and golden sands below.

Farewell, farewell my own true love. The time has come
    to go,

Goodbye to Ballybunion where the Shannon waters flow.

I walk along a sandy shore beside a silver sea,

Where every wave and ripple there remind me love of
    thee.

And when at night the stars are bright beside the pale
    moon's glow,

I'll dream of Ballybunion and the Buds of long ago.

(Suddenly the Boozer appears with a loud roar right on top of them. They scatter shrieking, although not before he has caught Mrs Black by the backside. He is left alone in triumph).

CURTAIN
for end of Act One.

ACT TWO

Scene One

Tom Shaun and Moon are seated in J. D.'s public house. Con and Molly are at another table. A barman stands behind the bar.

Tom: My father used to sit here. Regularly at eight every night he took up his position in this exact spot. He'd be joined by others from time to time. They would consume their quotas and pass on or pass out as the case might be. As for himself, one and one half bottles of Paddy Flaherty whiskey was the minimum nightly intake. On festive occasions he was known to polish off two full bottles, or to break it down, two score half ones of unwatered whiskey.

Moon: A nice cargo.

Tom: A nice cargo indeed.

Moon: Tell me was he ever drunk?

Tom: Never. It was not in the power of whiskey to make that man drunk. Not a blink nor a wink from him, not a stagger not a swagger. Full to the gills he might be but you'd never hear a burp nor a belch nor a groan out of him, or any revelation whatsoever high or low from the posterior.

Moon: Remarkable!

Tom: Truly remarkable. Back to the lodgings then for the nightly caper and that man would dance for you and prance for you till the rest of the world was fit for nothing but the bed.

Moon: A supernatural man.

Tom: Oh a pure hoor of a man.

Moon: But he's dead Tom.

Tom: There's no need to tell me that. Everyone knows

40

that.

Moon: Everyone except you Tom.

Tom: What are you talking about?

Moon: The truth Tom. The cold clear truth. You're a rake Tom. A decent one but still a rake.

Tom: For God's sake man that's known to all.

Moon: You refuse to let go of your father's hand.

Tom: It's no harm surely to talk about him.

Moon: No harm at all but you Tom talk about nothing else. Do you not ever think of a nice woman? A woman, for instance, like Mary O'Dea?

Tom: Shh! Someone will hear you.

Moon: So you do think about her, nice and cuddlesome eh Tom? Snug in your arms no doubt in the grey of the cool morning or the black of the lonely night.

Tom: God's sake man someone will hear you. What's coming over you at all.

Moon: She likes you Tom.

Tom: In the name of God what would a woman like that see in an oul' tearaway like me?

Moon: She sees promising clay Tom, clay that could be moulded into a worthwhile man.

Tom: You don't know what you're talking about.

Moon: It's your father isn't it?

Tom: Nonsense.

Moon: Your father never bothered with a woman after your mother died and you imitating his lofty example did likewise. You think I don't see the guilt in your face when you look at Mary O'Dea?

Tom: God's sake will you cut it out.

Moon: The same guilt is in every honest man that ever looked at a woman but in your case there's more to it than that. Isn't there?

Tom: I don't know what you mean.

Moon: Don't you Tom?

Tom: How could I ever look Mary O'Dea straight in the

face. I have lost all right to the love of a woman long ago.

Moon: But you think of her?

Tom: Lord God, do I what? I think or nothing else but she's away above and beyond the likes of me.

Moon: You do love her?

(Tom nods).

Moon: Really love her? *(Tom nods again)* Good. I'm old Tom. My days are numbered. Death will knock on my door any day now.

Tom: But you don't care. You're ready. You have no fear of death.

Moon: Of course no fear but never mind about me Tom. It's you're the man. The time has come Tom to face reality. Mary O'Dea is alive. Her voice sings with the richness of the love she has to give. I wish I was young enough to take advantage of it myself. Don't let that love go to waste. If you do it will be the worst sin of all.

Tom: No. No. I can't. It's out of the question, there's no hope for a fellow like me. No hope at all. I'm only a tearaway.

Moon: There is hope Tom. There's always hope for a man with love in his heart.

Con: Is the sherry to your liking my dear?

Molly: It's being with you Con my love that makes the sherry sweet.

Con: How you always lift my heart my dearest one with everything you say and do.

Molly: How much more time have we Con?

Con: Let us put time to one side for the rest of this night my love. Let us pretend that our parting will never be, that we'll be here, side by side, in this place we love forever and forever.

Molly: Of course Con darling. I'll pretend anything you want if it makes you happy.

Con: How kind you are. How unselfish.

Molly: It's you who are kind, who always has been kind through thick and thin. Whenever I awake and see your face beside me the day brightens my love.

Con: It brightens for me too.

Molly: Do you think they know about us?

Con: Who?

Molly: The people at O'Deas.

Con: All they know is what they see and hear. What they see is a pair of old sweethearts and what they hear are sweet words of love.

Molly: That's so true. I sometimes wonder Con. Oh look there's Mr Moon.

Con: He's been there awhile. He's the sharpest of all is Moon and yet even he knows nothing. Let's go.

(They bid good evening to Tom and Moon. Exit both).

Moon: Don't ask me why but I've always sensed something fishy about that pair. Always collaborating and conspiring so sweetly. Like a honeymoon couple for all their years. You would think one would feel the need to escape the other for awhile now and then but no. They can't bear to be without each other for a moment of the day. Too close. Far too close. Far too close for comfort if you ask me.

CURTAIN
for end of Scene 1, Act 2.

ACT TWO

Scene Two

The scene changes to the kitchen. Here the ladies are knitting.

Mrs Black: Did ye see the lady in the strand today with the two-piece bathing suit and her belly as bare as a new-born babe's?

Mrs Bunce: Oh yes I saw her. That was a disgraceful exhibition altogether.

Mrs Black: Did you see the men watching her? Old as well as young.

Mrs Bunce: The old men are the worst of all. They watch with hungrier eyes.

Mrs Black: Old men are very las-kiv-ious.

Tessie: Worst of all I fear hairy men.

Bessie: She has hairy men on the brain.

Molly: You may be sure Con Somers wasn't watching her. He has something better to do with his time.

Mrs Black: Well now I'm sure I never said Con Somers was watching her.

Mary: Of course Con wasn't. Con is a gentleman.

Tessie: I'm sure that girl will have neither luck nor grace making a show of herself like that.

Mrs Black: No woman should reveal more than her head, her hands and her two bare feet.

Mrs Bunce: True for you Mrs Black. My mother always said that not an inch should be revealed from the collar up and the breastbone down.

Mrs Black: I declare to God you wouldn't make a decent handkerchief from what that girl was wearing. And did

44

you see the strut of her, parading herself for all to see.

Mrs Bunce: Hush, hush. The men are here.

(Enter Tom, Moon and Con. They stand around).

Mrs Black: Would you like a seat nearer the fire Con?

Con: No thank you Mrs Black. I'm happy where I am.

Tom: Did you see the yoke on the beach today?

Moon: A shameless rip although they say that if you go around half naked it helps the circulation.

Tom: Her circulation now or yours?

Moon: I'm long gone from that kind of thing.

Tom: I don't know. They say the urge remains until a man is seven days dead. Did you see her today Con?

Con: You mean the girl with the bikini?

Moon: Is that what they call it?

Con: I am not referring to *it* as you call it. I am referring to the garment she was wearing.

Moon: Ah!

Con: It's called a bikini after the island of the same name which is part of the Marshall Islands in the Pacific Ocean. It would be seven minutes past four in the afternoon there now.

Tom: And she'd be still in her bikini.

Moon: And that's all they wear there?

Con: It's the climate.

Moon: A boult of cloth would go a long way there Tom.

Con: She was a fine looking girl.

Moon: I didn't think you would notice such things Con.

Con: Why not?

Tom: Why not indeed?

Moon: In case Molly there would be keeping an eye on you.

Mary: Isn't anybody going to sing tonight or dance or tell a story?

Dolly: A story is what I want and Tom Shaun is the man to tell it.

Tom: Now how could anyone refuse a story when Dolly O'Dea is in the asking of it?

45

Con: Good man Tom.

Mary: Silence all now while Tom Shaun tells a story.

Tom: In the townland of Acushna in north Kerry there was a widow woman with three daughters. She was obliged to send the eldest daughter into service with a strong farmer who lived more than twenty miles away in a fertile plain. The girl's name was Bridgie Malgoorie and her age was fifteen. She didn't remember her dead father but she spoke to him often when she was afraid or when she was alone. She settled into work in jig time and the farmer and his wife were well pleased with her for whatever else she might fear she had no fear of hard work. But then one night a sad thing happened. It was this way. Christmas Eve was the time and outside the snow was overcoating the hills and decorating the limbs of the bare trees. Bridgie was about to turn into the hollow of sleep when the door of the room opened silently and the farmer stood framed in it. Hush girl said he. Hush and there'll be no one the wiser from what transpires between us. Bridgie slipped out of the bed praying to the good God and His Blessed Mother to protect her. She ran past the farmer in her nightdress, down the stairs. Come back. Come back he called after her in sorrow. Come back. I'm sorry. I'll do you no harm. But it was too late. Out in the night the snow had stopped but now it was freezing hard and the cold of the road benumbed poor Bridgie's feet. Then she heard footsteps approaching from behind her. She drew into the roadside bushes in terror and waited for the footsteps to pass. . . but pass they did not. A tall man wearing a long, grey coat stood with his hands outstretched and motioned her to come into his arms. She looked into the man's face and she knew at once she was safe from all harm. The man opened his great coat and buttoned it round her. She never felt so warm or so cosy or so comfortable in her life before. Off they went, while the tall man whistled that stately hornpipe known as *The Blackbird*. After a while she fell asleep in his arms and when she opened her eyes again she found herself standing alone outside her mother's door. That was the welcome they gave her. That was the celebrating and crying and laughing and dancing on that happy Christmas morning. But how? asked her mother. How did you come? I met a tall man said Bridgie. Had he a pale face asked her mother and had he curly black hair? He had indeed said Bridgie. And had he a grey coat and did he whistle *The Blackbird?* Yes. Yes said Bridgie. Then said her mother that man who brought you home safe was your own dead father.

Dolly: Did it really happen?

Tom: It happened. I knew the girl well. She went to America in the finish when all fruit failed in her own neck of the wood.

Tessie: I'll bet that farmer was a hairy man.

Mary: After a sad story like that I think a dance would be the very thing.

Moon: Yes now for a dear old dance. Now for a stately waltz. Mary my darling will you endeavour to drag me round the floor.

(All rise and prepare themselves).

Dolly: I hereby declare this waltz a lady's choice and you Tom Shaun are the one I choose.

Tom: Well now Dolly you'd wait many a day to meet a worse dancer than me. Still I'm game if you are. 'Tis your toes that's in danger, not mine.

Con: May I have the pleasure of this dance madam?

Molly: You may indeed I'm sure kind sir.

(All waltz. Mary and Dolly sing each verse, others repeat it).

BALLYBUNION SONG

I walk along a sandy shore beside a silver sea,
Where every wave and ripple there reminds me love of thee.

And when at night the stars are bright beside the pale
  moon's glow,
I'll dream of Ballybunion and the loves of long ago.

I'll dream of Ballybunion and the lonely castle there,
The seabirds crying overhead, high in the scented air.
And so farewell my own true love, the time has come to
  go,
Goodbye to Ballybunion and the loves of long ago.

Dolly: Mr Moon will you be my next partner?

Moon: You flatter me Dolly and I'm truly sorry but my
  next partner is going to be my bed.

Mary: The night is only starting Mr Moon.

Con: Aren't you afraid to go to bed some night and never
  wake up?

Tom: I never saw a man so devoted to the early bed.

Con: It wouldn't do for me. Bed can be a lonely spot —
  unless, of course, you have someone with you.

Tom: Would you ever be afraid in bed?

Moon: Afraid of what?

Con: Afraid you might never wake up?

Moon: That never worries me. I have a clear conscience.
  I'm ready to go when I'm called.

Tom: I'd want to go to confession every day before my
  conscience grew any way clear.

Mrs Black: Do you go to confession every day Mr Moon?

Moon: Indeed I don't — I have something better to do with
  my time.
  (Looks are exchanged).

Mrs Black: Once a week then Mr Moon?

Moon: No, nor once a month.

Tom: He's a once a year man like myself.

Moon: No I'm not. I haven't been inside a confession box
  in twenty years.
  (Gasps of astonishment).

Mrs Black: Lord bless and save us all! *(Blessing herself).*

Mrs Bunce: Amen.

Moon: I have no notion of telling the story of my life to some backward farmer's son with a roundy collar on him. *(Gasps)* Anyway, what sins could I commit now? I've forgotten how to curse and swear, I haven't enough money to get drunk and I'm too weak to go with a woman. No sir. No confession for me. Many's the night I said to my maker, 'I'm ready to go whenever you are.' You'll never hear me whine for a priest. Goodnight all.

CURTAIN
for end of Scene 2, Act 2.

ACT TWO

Scene Three

Moon in bed. Enter a sleek, nattily-dressed figure with walking cane, polished and articulate. This is Death. He looks at Moon and then introduces himself; or Death may be a voice offstage.

Death: My name is death. *(Laughs)* You expected something else, something uncommon, out of the ordinary. Alas my dear people there is nothing as common as death. Everybody has a perfect right to it. *(Touches Moon with walking stick)* Wake up there. *(To audience)* Correct me if I'm wrong but this is the chap who says he's not worried about meeting me? *(To Moon)* Wake up Moon. I've come for you.

Moon: (Sitting up in bed) Who is it? Who's that? *(Notices Death)* Who are you?

Death: Don't you know me?

Moon: Should I?

Death: Of course you should. I am death.

Moon: (Clutches throat) Oh God! Not that, not that. *(Pulls clothes over head).*

Death: Come, come now. Remember what you always say, we come and we go. How quaint that is. We come and we go.

Moon: (Casts clothes aside) Go away. Go away. Leave me alone. Go . . . Leave at once.

Death: I can't Nothing personal mind you. Just get it into your mind that I cannot leave . . . on my own.

Moon: Why? Why can't you?

Death: You know why. Come on now be a man and get ready.

Moon: No. No. No. No.

Death: Come on. If everybody behaved like that we'd never get anybody dead.

Moon: No. No.

Death: And I have so many people depending on me Moon — undertakers, florists — grave diggers. I have others to visit this night. I haven't all that time to waste on you.

Moon: No! No!

Death: For you're neither a great saint or a great sinner, Moon. You know that, don't you Moon?

Moon: Yes. I mean no.

Death: Then come on.

Moon: No! No!

Death: What's that other one of yours? Ah yes. 'The life I have loved so well will shortly abandon me callously and mercilessly to suit its own cycle.' And how's that you finished off? It took a brave man to say it. 'I wouldn't give you a solitary cockle shell for what's left of my life.' Bravely spoken Moon. Bravely spoken.

Moon: God's sake I didn't mean that. It was pure bravado. No man in his right mind would say a thing like that.

Death: But it's a cant with you.

Moon: It's meaningless. It's just words. Now please, I beg of you go away. I'm an old man. I need my sleep.

Death: Face the truth Moon for the first time in your life and, of course, the last time.

Moon: Wha. . . what do you mean?

Death: I can't go without you. I have my orders. It's as simple as that.

Moon: Go away will you.

Death: I can't.

Moon: But I'm not ready.

Death: If I got a penny for every time I heard that I'd be a millionaire.

Moon: Give me a little more time at least. Let me ready myself for the judgement.

Death: But why do you always say you don't care then?

Moon: I say it to hide my horror at the thought of you. I think of nothing else lately. I cringe, I tremble. I soil myself — my bed — at the awful prospect of going away with you. I'm a liar, a bluffer, a boaster.

Death: Ah!

Moon: I live in horror as my time grows shorter.

Death: Here's your hat. Let's get out of here.

Moon: No. No. Never. I'll never go with you.

Death: You can't escape it. There's no way out.

Moon: Look. I'll tell you what. Give me a few days. I'll never pretend I don't care again. You won't catch me bandying your name about I assure you. Give me another while. I need time. I have to make a good confession. My soul is black with sin.

Death: Confession? I thought you scorned confession.

Moon: I don't want to go to hell.

Death: Oh me, oh my! Hell, Heaven, Limbo, Purgatory, Fiddlers' Green. These are all inventions, mythological place names. I am the only thing that's real. I'm it Moon. The rest is sham. I am the only fact. I really exist. Look at the graveyards alone. Every tombstone is testimony to my power. Chin up now, hat on. Time to go.

Moon: (Shouting) Help! Help! Please somebody help! *(Moon falls out of bed and Death fades off. Enter Tom in a hurry).*

Tom: It's alright. It's me Mr Moon. Your friend. It's Tom Shaun.

Moon: Oh Tom am I glad to see you. I've had an awful time. He was here. He was right here.

Tom: Who was here?

Moon: Death Tom. He very nearly carried me off.

Tom: That was your imagination.

Moon: No. No. I tell you he was here. Look he cut my wrist.

Tom: No. No Mr Moon that was your own doing. You

52

were struggling with yourself. You were fighting with your conscience.

Moon: But I saw him Tom.

Tom: There was nobody here but yourself. That's the simple truth.

Moon: But I saw him as plain as the day, as plain as I see you now. He dragged me from the bed. What else would I be doing on the floor Tom?

Tom: Look Mr Moon. I've had nights like this. So has every mother's son. It's all over now. Come on. There's nothing to fear anymore. I'll be in the kitchen. You say your prayers now and the sleep will come. They'll bring you peace of mind.

Moon: My prayers Tom?

Tom: Your prayers old friend. That's what went wrong. Your forgot to say your prayers.

CURTAIN
for end of Scene 3, Act 2.

ACT TWO

Scene Four

The kitchen where Buds are dancing Patsy Healy type Mazurka. They pause, winded.

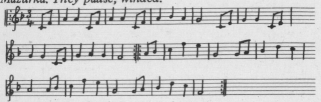

Con: I think now in all fairity that's enough dancing for one night.

All: Oh!

Con: My feet are killing me.

Molly: You can steep them before we go to bed.

Mrs Bunce: But it's too early for bed.

Mrs Black: And too late for a round of the village.

Bessie: Let's have a game of cards.

Molly: The very thing.

Mrs Black: Cards is a sin. I wouldn't contambulate myself with them.

Mrs Bunce: Not a harmless old game of twenty-five.

Mrs Black: Shame on you Mrs Bunce with knitting to do.

Mrs Bunce: Oh very well!

Con: Let's get this table back in place. The deck? Get the deck. There can be no cards without the deck.

Tom: It would be best I think if we played partners. Are you having a hand Mary?

Mary: Not yet thank you Tom. I must prepare for tomorrow.

Tessie: Count me out too. I have a touch of a pain in the

head. A turn in the garden won't do me any harm. *(Exit)*.

Con: Is she alright?

Bessie: Ah, don't worry — she gets like that sometimes. I'll go and see that she's alright. *(Exit)*.

Tom: That leaves four of us. Let a lady deal.

Dolly: I'm your lady.

Con: We will cast knaves for partners.

Tom: The Lord be good to my father he was the greatest card-player of all time. He could memorise the four suits from ace to king and tell you with his eyes closed what card was coming next.

Con: An extraordinary man. Me and you are partners Molly.

Tom: Extraordinary isn't the word for him. He once sat in a game of poker for seventy nine hours non-stop, drank thirteen bottles of whiskey and stood up in the latter end winning to the exact tune of ninety four pounds, seventeen shillings and sixpence.

Con: Amazing, amazing. Ah . . . Mrs Black will you partner Mrs Bunce?

Mrs Black: No! No! She is not. *(Drags Mrs Bunce off. Mary shrugs and follows)*.

Con: Well that leaves Dolly partnering Tom Shaun.

Dolly: What'll we play?

Con: We'll play twenty-five if all are agreed.

Dolly: How much will we play for?

Con: We'll play for the princely sum of a halfpenny per person. All outstanding debts to be honoured at the conclusion of each game.

Tom: I second that. Spin the wheel Dolly and let the great gamble begin.

Fade to Scene 5.

ACT TWO

Scene Five

The Boozer Malone is sauntering about. He pauses and faces audience.

Boozer: Bessie is gone in search of Tessie but Tessie poor thing is gone back to her wedding night, the night she left her husband, poor Murt Glug without consummating the marriage. Originally, of course, the marriage was one of agricultural convenience, in other words, it was a match. It opened the way for her brother Font to bring in his own wife. On that memorable night, Tessie walked five miles across the countryside, dragging her heavy suitcase after her until she reached home.

(Exit the Boozer. Enter Tessie wearing her dishevelled wedding outfit which includes a pink bonnet and high-heeled shoes. Wearily she drags suitcase after her. She knocks at front door having first plucked up the courage).

Tessie: *(She knocks at door)* Font? Font? Let me in.

(She knocks again. There is no response. She locates a pebble and throws it at upstairs window. There is still no response. She locates a second pebble and throws it at window. A tousled Font in nightshirt sticks out his head).

Tessie: Thank God you woke Font.

Font: I was sound. 'Twas all that drink at the wedding. But what are you doing here? You're supposed to be in your husband's house.

Tessie: I know. I know. I've had a terrible time. It was hell.

Font: What are you doing here?

Tessie: I couldn't stay there. It was terrible.

Font: What was terrible?

Tessie: I can't tell you.

56

Font: Well you better bloody well tell me.

Tessie: I can't. I can't tell anybody.

Font: You go back to your husband right away. There's no place here for you anymore.

Tessie: I'm sorry Font. There's no going back.

Font: It's no bloody use being sorry. That won't get me a woman in my bed.

Tessie: I know Font. I know. I know all that believe me.

Font: Jaze Tessie I'm nearly forty years of age. It's my last chance. You can't stay here now. Them days are gone. You made a deal. You stick to it. You can't stay here.

Tessie: I can't go back. I couldn't go through with it. I couldn't. I couldn't.

Font: You made a bargain. In the sight of God you made a bargain.

Tessie: I don't care what I made.

Font: Holy Saint Patrick you don't care and me desperate. Me out of my bloody wits for a woman of my own. Well by God I'll make you care. You're going back if I have to carry you.

Tessie: I am not.

Font: You're going back otherwise you'll wreck everything.

Tessie: I'm going to my own bed. I am never going back to that bed or that house.

Font: Take it easy now, just a minute or two, take it handy. Tell me exactly what happened. I have every right to know. Will you answer me or will I go down and shake the truth out of you... what happened?

Tessie: That's just it. Nothing happened.

Font: What do you mean?

Tessie: Exactly what I say.

Font: You mean you didn't go to bed with him?

Tessie: I went to bed with him but nothing happened because I didn't stay in bed, because the minute he tried to put his hands on me I jumped out of it.

Font: What did he say to that?

Tessie: Nothing. He turned over on his side.

Font: Why didn't you accommodate him?

Tessie: Because there was a rank smell off him.

Font: Sure jaze we all smell. Me, you, everybody.

Tessie: He has a smell from his breath and some of his teeth were black. He was dirty and greasy, swarthy and ugly and I was sick, sick, when I saw him exposed on the bed. He was hairy and matted like an ape. I couldn't bring myself to look at him a second time.

Font: So he was hairy? Well that was because he's a man you eejit. Men are hairy. Do you hear me, Tessie. Men are hairy.

Tessie: I didn't think they'd be as hairy as that. How could I? I've never seen a man like that before.

Font: Oh come on. You know what a man is. You've seen them in bathing togs in those magazines you and Bessie buy.

Tessie: Of course I have. I'm not denying that.

Font: Was that what you expected? A nice, pink, blue-eyed fellow with his hair creased and slicked but without a rib of hair on his damned body like that grinning bast-ard of a Swede with his big horse's teeth and no trace of hair at all? Well they weren't men you eejit, they were models. They get paid to tease ignoramuses like you. All their hair is singed off before they get their photos took. Was that the golden boy you dreamed of?

Tessie: Certainly not!

Font: Why did you spend so long looking at him?

Tessie: I don't know.

Font: You don't know? You bloody women can't admit an honest thought. Listen carefully to me Tessie. Murt Glug is no model. He has no time. He's rough and ready but he's honest and dacent. He wouldn't blackguard a woman if she played her cards right. He has his cattle and his land to tend. He has to keep on the go the whole time to make a living. Why didn't you close your eyes you silly bitch and pretend he was the golden fellow like a thousand women before you did? Make up your mind. You're going back.

Tessie: I'm not.

Font: I'll beat the daylights out of you if you don't.

Tessie: You can beat me to death for all I care.
(*Enter Bessie*).

Bessie: What in God's name is this? What happened Tess?

Tessie: I couldn't face him Bessie. Honestly I couldn't. He was rotten.

Font: If she's not back with her husband in the morning I'll kick her back.

Bessie: You leave her alone. You're to blame for all this.

Font: Me?

Bessie: You couldn't get her out quick enough. You didn't care as long as you had this place to yourself. What happened to her was of no importance. She wasn't ready for this. She's shy. . . she's sensitive. You wouldn't know that, of course.

Font: Maybe not but I have you figured alright. By God you would have made a better fist of that job tonight. You wouldn't be put off by a hairy chest.

Bessie: Go on Tessie. I won't be a minute. *(Exit Tessie)* I heard what you said. I'm not sure I fully understand what you mean.

Font: You know what I mean alright. If the cap fits you can wear it.

Bessie: In this case I'm pretty sure the cap doesn't.

Font: That's not what John Calvey says.

Bessie: What does John Calvey say?

Font: That you're the right sport in a hayshed.

Bessie: That's because I wouldn't allow him see me home from a dance once.

Font: So you say.

Bessie: If what he said were true he'd be far too cunning to advertise it. Even you must see that.

Font: What about Murt Glug? What about me?

Bessie: I'm sorry. I really am.

Font: Sorry you're a virgin is it... Sorry you can't see your way to marrying some poor oul' backward fellow like me, like Murt Glug? That's the truth of the matter isn't it? We're not good enough for our own women. They've gone from us to the towns and the cities to work as servants, servants when they could be mistresses right here.

Bessie: Well, follow them. It's not too late.

Font: You're joking. What would I do in a city or town? I'm a small farmer. I'm no good at anything else. I can't leave my livelihood. I'd starve without it.

Bessie: I'm going to bed.

Font: Oh yeah! That'll solve everything won't it. Into bed and pull the clothes over your head. Good God, look at me! Here I am saddled with two virgins and no hope of a wife.

Bessie: Goodnight. *(Exit).*

Font: Oh goodnight! Goodnight she says and that's the end of it. A land of virgins and lunatics. That's what we've got here. Virgins and bloody lunatics.

CURTAIN

for end of Scene 5, Act 2.

ACT TWO

Scene Six

The kitchen, same night. The card game is still in progress. Mary sits by the fire knitting. Enter Tessie and Bessie followed by Mrs Bunce and Mrs Black.

Mary: Sit by the fire ladies. I'll be making a cup of tea after the Rosary. Dolly see if Mr Moon's awake. Maybe he'd like a cup of tea.

Dolly: Yes mother. *(Dolly is about to exit towards left as Moon enters)* Why he's here.

Moon: I couldn't sleep. Is there a cup of tea going Mary?

Mary: I would have brought the tea to your bed Mr Moon.

Moon: No need for that Mary. I just had to get up.

Mary: Are you alright?

Moon: Yes . . . I'm alright now — but I think I'll call down to see the priest in the morning.

Mary: We're all here I believe.

Tom: Yes. Everybody's present and correct.

Mary: Before you kneel I have something to say and this, I think, is as good a time as any to say it. I don't know where to begin or how to put it but I'm afraid it's not good news. I could have waited till you were all going home. The truth is that yesterday I received a letter from the firm of solicitors who represent the landlords of this building. It's not the first letter I've received but this recent letter, unfortunately, is an ultimatum. I have been given notice to quit.

Tom: Never. We'll never submit to a demand like that.

Mary: I'm afraid there's nothing to be done. They are quite legally within their rights. I should have gone long ago.

Tom: Would money be any good? We could all help. Mr

61

Moon? Con?

Con: Yes. Yes I'll help.

Moon: I'll do my bit.

Mary: It's not as simple as that. The owners have plans to turn the place into a fun palace. The Atlantic Fun Palace.

Mrs Bunce: What?

Mrs Black: Oh my God!

Tom: Our last refuge.

Molly: But that would ruin the place.

Bessie: Poor Ballybunion.

Con: I'll have the law on them.

Moon: But they are the law.

Tom: But can they, just like that, do this?

Moon: If they have the law on their side they can do anything.

Molly: You mean it's all over? Our coming here year after year is all over?

Mary: I'm afraid so Molly.

Molly: This is the end of the world.

Mary: It's not as bad as that.

Molly: (In tears) Oh it is, it is. It is.

Con: There's a long story here. It will have to be told but now is not the time.

Bessie: But what are they going to give us back?

Moon: You don't seem to understand my dear.

Bessie: But I do. All I'm asking is what they propose to give us in return for the things they will be taking away from us.

Dolly: Now, now it's not as if we were being evicted. There will be goodwill money I'm sure for mammy and none of you will have any difficulty in finding other accommodation.

Bessie: That isn't so.

Con: Bessie's right. It isn't so and I'll tell you why. Nobody wants the Budderies anymore. We're looked upon as nuisances with our cabbages and spuds and eggs and bacon and our countrified comings and goings. We're out of step. This house was the last refuge of the Buds and now it's no more.

Mary: But you'll have guesthouses, hotels.

Con: It's not the same.

Bessie: Ours was a whole way of life. It was a culture in itself. That's why I ask what they propose to give us in return?

Mary: I'm afraid they're not obliged to give you anything Miss Nix.

Bessie: So with one letter, a solicitor's letter, they can annihilate us. Destroy our songs and dances and stories, a way of life that has been ours for generations?

Moon: Indeed that's true. There were Buds coming here when I was a boy and they were coming when I was a man.

Bessie: But they are killing the whole ritual of our living. Surely they should be made to pay?

Moon: Progress as they call it is as blind as a bat and as deaf as a stone and just as unfeeling as the concrete which accompanies it. Ballybunion will never be the same.

Tom: For us, no, but for the younger generation that looks for noise and excitement and all things new. It's Dolly's world now — we had our fling.

Bessie: It's wrong, we should have a say in what becomes of us.

Moon: It's another world Miss Bessie. Not ours anymore, somebody else's turn now.

Tom: And you'll get nothing back Miss Bessie, none of us will.

Bessie: But we should, we should. If there was any justice we should. They snatch away our life and what do they hand us? Pinballs and roulettes and blaring noise that would deafen a body and this is only the start. They'll take more and more and more in the name of progress

63

but they'll put nothing of value back. They never do.

Moon: It's all part of the new world. It's what people want.

Molly: Well it's not what I want. It's not what I want.

(She cries out loud. Con consoles her).

Mary: Can I help Con?

Con: No thank you Mary. This is something that calls for thought. We, myself and this woman, have been struck a terrible blow this night. Our little world is after collapsing around our ears. Come on my pet. We'll keep our heads high no matter what.

(Exit Con and Molly).

Mary: I never dreamed it would affect them like that.

Moon: Remember Mary they've been coming here for the greater part of their lives and what did I always say to you Tom? There's more to them than meets the eye.

Mrs Black: 'Tis a terrible blow to us all. It was our refuge and our hope.

Tessie: What will we do at all?

Tom: What will you do Mary?

Mary: I'll be alright Tom. As long as God leaves me these two hands I'll be alright. Now we'll all kneel down and say the Rosary. At least we have that much left to us after the day. Will you lead off Mr Moon?

(All kneel facing audience across stage).

Moon: Am I worthy to lead you good people?

Mary: Of course you are.

Moon: Incline unto my aid O God.

All: Oh Lord make haste to help me.

Moon and All: Glory be to the Father, the Son and the Holy Ghost.

Moon: Our Father Who Art in Heaven etc.,

All: Give us this day our daily bread etc.,

(Spot on Widows as prayers go on).

Mrs Black: What will we do now? Our sanctuary's gone forever?

Mrs Bunce: Pray harder than we ever prayed before. There's no other course open to us.

Mrs Black: 'Tis a terrible blow. Notice to quit at our age.

Mrs Bunce: Pray. Remember God never closes one door
without opening another.
(Spot on Nixes).

Bessie: I still can't get used to the idea.

Tessie: I can't believe it's never to open again. What will we
do?

Bessie: We'll think of something. God is good.

Tessie: But what about Font?

Bessie: What about him?

Tessie: You know he brings in a woman while we're away.

Bessie: Yes. I've noticed her touches here and there.

Tessie: What is to happen now?

Bessie: Perhaps we should stay away.

Tessie: Forever?

Bessie: It might be best.

Tessie: But how? Where?

Bessie: Shhh . . . Pray. There's always a way. Just pray.
*(Spot on Dolly and Moon. Mary leads off with the Our
Father).*

Dolly: What's going to happen to you Mr Moon?

Moon: I'll be alright Dolly. No need to worry about me,
not anymore.

Dolly: What about Tom Shaun?

Moon: We'll have to do something drastic in that respect
and we'll have to do it soon.

Dolly: What do you suggest?

Moon: You'll have to put your cards on the table.

Dolly: You think he might . . . .

Moon: I think there would be no holding him back if you
could get him started but getting him started isn't going
to be easy.

Dolly: I'll get him started.

Moon: That's the spirit. Just remember whenever he baulks
that you mother is the highest thought in his head. Now

65

let's pray for what we want.

Tom: Notice to quit! Poor Mary — what a blow for her and what will it mean to me? Could it mean that I will never lay eyes on Mary O'Dea again? That surely would be purgatory enough for any sinner. Not to see her ever again. That wouldn't be purgatory, that would be hell! Sheer hell!

Mary: Hail Mary full of grace etc.,

All: Holy Mary Mother of God pray for us sinners etc., *(Lights fade).*

CURTAIN

for end of Act Two.

ACT THREE

Scene One

Front of lodging house the second last morning of September. Mary has a bunch of flowers in her hand.

Dolly: Another lovely morning mam. It is like as if it was specially designed to say goodbye to the Buds. You'd never think it was the second last day of September.

Mary: Yes Dolly — the second last day.

Dolly: And we really have to leave tomorrow?

Mary: No way out now, I'm afraid. *(Sits on seat).*

Dolly: Are you sorry to be leaving Mam?

Mary: We can never depend on life staying the same Dolly. We have to make the best of what it has to offer, but I am sorry. I've spent all my life here.

Dolly: I'm sorry for the Buds, most of all that we'll never see them again. They always seemed so simple and uncomplicated, compared to the people we get here during the summer — but they weren't really mam were they? Mr Moon, the Nix ladies, Mrs Bunce and Mrs Black, Con and Molly — they've been very glum over these last days — and what about Tom Shaun — especially Tom Shaun?

Mary: People just seem simple and uncomplicated Dolly. They seldom are. The Buds like everybody else have their problems too. Now why don't you go for a nice stroll along the strand, say goodbye to your friends.

Dolly: Sure. And don't worry Mam. I'm sure things will work out alright — and, you know, I could get a job.

Mary: We'll manage love — off with you now while the sun is high.

(Enter Father Bunce).

Dolly: Good morning father.

67

Fr Bunce: Morning Dolly, Mary.

Mary: Morning father. *(Exit Dolly).*

Fr Bunce: You leave tomorrow?

Mary: On the bus tomorrow evening.

Fr Bunce: Have you decided upon something?

Mary: I've answered some ads. Cooks are always in demand. I should have no trouble really.

Fr Bunce: And Dolly?

Mary: Dolly will be part of the bargain.

Fr Bunce: When she grows up and leaves you?

Mary: I've faced worse loss. It's not like she'd be gone forever.

Fr Bunce: Ah! Flowers I see.

Mary: I'm paying a visit to the graveyard Father. Heaven knows when I'll see his grave again.

Fr Bunce: Ah, yes — his grave!

Mary: What about your mother?

Fr Bunce: What about her?

Mary: Can you do something for her?

Fr Bunce: I cannot interfere. I've advised her time and again but she was always heedless of what I said.

Mary: She needs help father.

Fr Bunce: I know.

Mary: The local parish priest needs a housekeeper. He's a nice man but I don't know him that well.

Fr Bunce: And I don't know him at all — he's new since last year.

Mary: But one priest to another?

Fr Bunce: I see. Maybe you have given me an idea however. I'll do my best Mary.

Mary: And so will I Father, you can count on that.

Fr Bunce: Mary . . . You'd make a man very happy. Don't you know that.

Mary: All I know Father is that my man is in his grave.
(She exits with flowers. He scratches his chin thinking.

68

Voice of Mrs Black is heard. He hurriedly returns to reading of his Office).

CURTAIN
for end of Scene 1, Act 3.

ACT THREE

Scene Two

Father Bunce continues with his Office. Enter Mrs Black and Mrs Bunce.

Mrs Black: 'Tis a beautiful morning Mrs Bunce but I'm sure 'twill rain.

Mrs Bunce: (Piously, sanctimoniously for Fr Bunce's benefit) There is no refuge like the refuge of prayer.

Mrs Black: Amen say I. Amen, amen, amen.

Mrs Bunce: Amen indeed for you may close your eyes and see only what you want to see. Hear only what you want to hear.

Mrs Black: And was there a question you were anxious to ask my dear?

Mrs Bunce: A question? Let me see. Ah! Tell me did Our Lord ever turn His back on His blessed mother?

Mrs Black: Never. Never in all His thirty-three years.

Mrs Bunce: Did He ever refuse her anything?

Mrs Black: Never.

Mrs Bunce: Thanks be to the Lord.

Mrs Black: Miracles He performed for her.

Mrs Bunce: Miracles for His mother.

Mrs Black: Sure didn't He change wine into water for her.

Mrs Bunce: And we only wanting a place of our own, any oul' hole to crawl into at the end of our days.

Mrs Black: At the end of our days and not many of them left God pity us! Maybe none at all.

Mrs Bunce: Wouldn't they be sorry then though.

Mrs Black: Too late then, but there is still time.

Mrs Bunce: Prayer is the answer. Prayer so that we might resign ourselves to the Holy Will of God. Prayer to blind us to the woes of the world.

Together: Prayer so that we might resign ourselves to the Holy Will of God. Prayer to blind us to the woes of the world.

(They exit triumphantly. Fr Bunce close book with a snap. Enter Con and Molly).

Con: Good morrow to you Father. *(Molly sobs).*

Fr Bunce: My dear Mrs Somers it's not the end of the world.

Molly: It's the end of our world Father.

Fr Bunce: But there are guesthouses and hotels and you have each other.

Molly: Have we Father? Have we Con? Have we each other?

Con: Now, now my love. You'll only upset yourself.

Molly: It's God's way of punishing us Father. We couldn't have luck. I always knew it would finish bad. Inside here in my heart I always knew.

Con: Oh dear! Oh dear! There's no consoling her since Mary O'Dea gave us the bad news. Things were bad enough before but that was the blow that brought us to our knees. Tomorrow is the last day, our last day Father.

Fr Bunce: What does she mean when she says you couldn't have luck?

Con: That's a long story Father but a story that must be told soon if we're ever to have the grace of God again.

Molly: Oh may God pity us. Our Lady intercede for us.

(Exit into house).

Fr Bunce: God is merciful. You must never forget that Mr Somers.

Con: He is Father but neighbours are not. Will you come with us now to know would we make a clean breast of a matter that's played on our consciences this many a long year.

Fr bunce: I'll go with you if that's what you wish but shouldn't we sit here first and talk things over.

Con: We'd appreciate that Father and perhaps you might not be hard on us yourself when our tale is told.

Fr Bunce: My calling doesn't allow me to be hard Con.
(Enter a swarthy, squat man with a broad-rimmed black hat, black coat and turned-down wellingtons. He is Murt Glug).

Murt: Where here would a man quarter a pony?

Con: Go to the back of any pub. There's outhouses galore. You can stable him where you like.

Murt: And tell me now is there oats to be had?

Con: If you have the price you'll get oats.

Fr Bunce: Don't I know you from somewhere?

Murt: You know me now whether you did or you didn't.

Fr Bunce: It's just that I thought we might have met.

Murt: Are you in the habit of going to the creamery?

Fr Bunce: No.

Murt: The bog?

Fr Bunce: No.

Murt: Do you spread manure?

Fr Bunce: No.

Murt: Do you scour dykes?

Fr Bunce: No.

Murt: Of course you don't no more nor I hears confession so 'tis hardly likely we met.

Fr Bunce: Hardly. Let's call it a case of mistaken identity then.

Murt: You're a country man by the looks of you.

Con: Correct.

Murt: Tell us is there a lodging house for Buds around here?

Con: By what name?

Murt: O'Dea, Mary O'Dea.

Con: Over there across the street. You can't miss it.

Murt: Maybe now 'tis how you stays there yourself?

Con: Maybe.

Murt: Is there by any chance a pair of prime heifers in lodgings there.

Con: Could be.

Murt: Ha — ha! Could be you say!

Con: Could be.

Murt: Name of Nix? One Bessie, the other Tessie?

Con: They're there.

Murt: God spare you the health.

Con: I think I know you.

Murt: What you know you know. What I know is that I have a pony to untackle and a woman to find.

Con: Do you answer to the name of Glug? Murt Glug?

Murt: Bulls-eye country man. Bulls-eye.

CURTAIN
for end of Scene 2, Act 3.

ACT THREE

Scene Three

Dolly is washing up. Enter Tom Shaun.

Dolly: Good morning Tom Shaun.

Tom: Morning Dolly. Where is everybody?

Dolly: Out. That's where.

Tom: Good God don't tell me that's the time of day!

Dolly: That's the time alright.

Tom: Am I the last?

Dolly: The very last. They've all had breakfast and been to Mass and gone to the strand. Everyone saving yourself. You'll have a cup of tea and toast. Would you like toast?

Tom: No thank you Dolly. Tea will do nicely. Seldom I sleep it out mind you.

Dolly: I am glad we're alone.

Tom: You are?

Dolly: Yes. I want to talk to you. First I'll set the table and then we'll have tea.

Tom: It would be more in my line to shave but, however, a mouthful of tea is no bad start to any day. Too much tea, of course, like too much of anything is bad. My father used always say that one good mug of tea going to bed was better than any sleeping pill. Of course, in his case now a pound of tea made no battle. He liked his brew as black as a famine spud. On top of that he used to chew tea leaves like an ordinary man would chew tobacco.

Dolly: Chew tea?

Tom: Chew tea. Signs on his teeth were as brown as bog-deal.

Dolly: You like it strong don't you?

74

Tom: Oh yes. Strong for me. Weak tea for weak people. My father, of course, would never buy his tea in pound packets like ordinary people.

Dolly: What way would he buy it then?

Tom: In a chest. A hundred weight at a time.

Dolly: What would he do if 'twas rationed like now?

Tom: He'd do without it. If he couldn't have a thing that was that.

Dolly: Now.

Tom: Now what?

Dolly: Now for our talk.

Tom: Yes. You did mention a talk. Well, as the saying goes, please to proceed.

Dolly: Yes. . .

Tom: Well?

Dolly: You know my mother well don't you?

Tom: I know her well enough I suppose.

Dolly: Do you like her?

Tom: Yes. Of course I do. Everybody likes her.

Dolly: I'm not talking about everybody. I'm talking about you.

Tom: I like her.

Dolly: How much?

Tom: How much what?

Dolly: How much do you like her?

Tom: A good bit.

Dolly: How much is a good bit?

Tom: I'd rather now you didn't ask me that.

Dolly: Why not?

Tom: Because that is a question of a personal nature. I just can't tell you that.

Dolly: But you must tell me.

Tom: Tell you what?

Dolly: Tell me how fond you are of my mother and stop avoiding the issue. Now answer. How fond are you of my mother?

Tom: Very. And that's all the information on that subject you're going to draw out of me.

Dolly: And what about me?

Tom: You?

Dolly: Yes me.

Tom: What about you?

Dolly: Are you fond of me?

Tom: Fond of you is it? My dear Dolly there is no sunbeam leaking in through that window as bright as you, no drewdrop of the dawn as dainty. I wouldn't give your small toe Dolly O'Dea for all the drink in Guinness's brewery and that's saying something. I wouldn't give your morning smile for all the diamonds in the mines of Kimberley and you ask me am I fond of you.

Dolly: Just talk like that to my mother and you'll have her swooning in no time.

Tom: Oh I could never talk like that to your mother. It's different with you. Everyone knows I'm fond of you.

Dolly: I'm fond of you too and my mind is made up. You, Tom Shaun Shea, are going to marry my mother. She'll be back any minute now. All you have to do is tell her you love her.

Tom: I can't do that. Let me out of here in God's name!

Dolly: Stand your ground.

Tom: In God's name let me go Dolly. I beg of you let me go. *(Seeks in vain to escape).*

Dolly: You're nothing but a great big cowardy custard. I'm ashamed of you. Now sit down there and listen. Do you love her?

Tom: Do I love her is it?

Dolly: Nod your head if you do. Shake it if you don't. *(After awhile he nods his head)* You must tell her.

Tom: I can't

Dolly: You must.

Tom: Never.

Dolly: My mother and I both need you Tom. Surely you're not going to leave us now that we have nothing.

Tom: No, no. Of course not. I wouldn't leave you. I'd never do that.

Dolly: Then you'll tell her?

Tom: Oh God help me!

Dolly: For my sake.

Tom: You don't know what you ask.

Dolly: Please. For me Tom.

Tom: How would I put it? What words would I use?

Dolly: Just walk up to her and say I want to tell you something. She'll say what and you say I love you.

Tom: I love you. Just that?

Dolly: Just that.

Tom: No more?

Dolly: No more. It's simple. That'll be her now.

Tom: Oh merciful God!

Dolly: This is your big chance. If you muff it I'll never speak to you again.

Tom: Could I send her a note?

Dolly: Oh no. No notes. It has to be straight to her face.
(Enter Mary).

Mary: Good morning Tom.

Tom: Good morning Mary.

Mary: You slept it out.

Tom: I did. I slept it out Mary.

Mary: You had some breakfast?

Tom: Oh yes. I had. I had some breakfast. I had indeed some breakfast. Aye. . .

Dolly: Tom has something to tell you mother. Haven't you Tom? I have things to be doing. I'll see you both later. Tom!
(Exit Dolly).

Mary: Well Tom and what have you to say?

77

Tom: What have I to say is it?

Mary: Yes. What have you to say? Dolly said there was something.

(Mary takes off her coat and moves off).

Tom: Did she? There's something alright. If 'twas my father now he'd grasp the bull by the horns. He'd smother her with words, words long, short and middling, words sweeter than honey, softer than eiderdown. By God but that man could let go a torrent of talk when 'twas wanted and to think he reared a dummy.

Mary: I'm waiting Tom. Well!

Tom: I was thinking of my father. He was a great talker. He could go on forever.

Mary: I'm sure he could.

Tom: Forever and ever.

Mary: But you yourself have nothing to say? Is that it?

Tom: Oh I have. I have.

Mary: Then say it.

Tom: Did you say, say it?

Mary: That's what I said.

Tom: I thought that was what you said.

Mary: Say it.

Tom: What'll I say?

Mary: Whatever it is you want to say.

Tom: It'll keep awhile. I'll wait till later on. That would be best I think. Later on.

Mary: I may not be here later on. I won't be here ever again.

Tom: Don't I know. Oh for God's sake who knows better.

Mary: Tomorrow we'll be all gone so if it's to be said Tom, whatever it is, it's best it be said now. There won't be any other time.

Tom: God be good to my father he used always say time and tide wait for no man.

Mary: I could not care less Tom what your father had to say about anything. In fact Tom I'm sick and tired of hearing about your father. Morning, noon and night we have quotations from him. In God's name don't you think it's time you said something of your own accord?

Tom: Sorry.

Mary: Sorry. Is that all you can say? You expect me to stand here wasting time listening to the same litany day in, day out. I know it by heart Tom. I know what your father had to say about every subject under the sun but I'll never know what you wanted to say to me because you're your father's parrot and as far as I can see all you'll ever be is a parrot. Now you must excuse me. I'm busy.

(Exit Mary to room nearby).

Tom: (To heavens) Father will you come to my aid. You hear what she called me, a parrot. It's all your fault. A parrot imagine! Come on. Infuse a bit of fire into me. Give me the courage to tell her what I think. This is my last chance man. If I don't sweep her off her feet in the next five minutes I'm doomed. You hear. Doomed because I can't bear the thought of growing old without her.

(He walks around, grinding his teeth, clenching and unclenching his fists, in desperate straits. He uplifts his hands and prays fervently).

Tom: Mary . . . Come down here. *(To himself)* It's now or never.

Mary: I can't. I'm busy.

Tom: Come down here Mary and come now. This very instant. This is a matter of life or death. Do you hear. . . a matter of life or death.

(Enter Mary).

Mary: What is it now? I'm up to my ears packing.

Tom: Stand there. Just stand there until I tell you the ways I love you. The first time is the morning when I awake. I gather myself and look about me to see where I am and then my heart starts to sing because I'm here in this house with you. Then I listen and your voice comes to me from the kitchen. You hum and you croon as you go about your morning's work and I can't wait to get downstairs to see the wonder of your morning face because inside me, Mary O'Dea, is a longing for you such as no man ever had for a woman and until the day comes when I can have you for my own I'll always be only the half of a man. Later as I walk the shore I see you everywhere. In the sky and the sea, in every horizon your face is there before me and that's the way it's been with me since the day I first set eyes on you and that's the way 'twill stay until I'm no more. I have never loved anybody, dreamed of anybody, desired anybody but you. That's all I wanted to say to you. You can go now.

Mary: I never knew. Why didn't you say something, anything?

Tom: I was afraid I'd lose your friendship. The gamble was too great.

Mary: And you stayed silent all this time.

Tom: All this time till now.

Mary: I don't know what to say.

Tom: You'll have to say yes or no. There can be no maybes after this. It has to be one way or the other. I've laid bare my heart.

Mary: Do you want to kiss me?

Tom: I do.

Mary: Kiss me then.
  (Enter Moon).

Moon: As you were, in God's name. Pretend I wasn't here at all. Please resume your former positions. Redouble your efforts. I'll be on my way.
  (Exit Moon).

Tom: Will you marry me? *(She nods, quite overcome)* Say it.

Mary: Yes Tom. I'll marry you. I'll have to break it to Dolly, of course.

Tom: No need for that. That's all been taken care of long before now.

Mary: Will you be able to support us?

Tom: Of course. There's a fine house and a good farm. A bit run down like myself but a woman's hand will rectify all.

Mary: I'm so happy Tom. It's so good to be loved, especially when it's a wonderful man like you.

Tom: Oh now, now there's nothing wonderful about me. But about you Mary, everything is more wonderful than the next.

Mary: Oh Tom. I'm not used to this. I'll die with the shame. You'll turn my head entirely.

Tom: There's a lot I'll be saying to you from this day out. Oh boy but will I be addressing myself to you in real earnest from now on. *(He takes her in his arms)* From now on you'll be spending a lot more of your time in here.

(Enter Tessie and Bessie. There is an embarrassing moment).

Mary: Won't you sit down girls.

Tom: Yes. Sit down. Sit down.

Mary: Dinner won't be for awhile yet ... but there's tea in the pot if you'd like a drop.

Tom: Wonderful, golden, well-drawn tea.

(Enter the Widows and Mr Moon. General excitement. Tom seats Widows and Nixes at table).

Tom: Sit down. Sit down. There's tea on the draw the like of which was never poured by mortal man. Nut brown tea from the land of Cathay, wet by the hand of Mary O'Dea.

Mrs Black: You're in a sprightly mood Mr Shea.

Tom: I have cause to be Mrs Black. I have cause to be.

Mrs Bunce: Maybe now 'tis a thing congratulations would be in order.

Tom: You're right as the rain Mrs Bunce. Congratulations

are in order. Very soon Mr Moon lovely Mary O'Dea will be Mrs O'Shea.

Moon: You lucky dog. *(Shakes his hands, kisses Mary)* I could not be more delighted Mary.

(Enter Murt Glug).

Murt: God save all here.

Tom: And you likewise. Who might you be sir?

Mary: Can we help you?

Murt: Some that's here knows who I am and knows what brings me.

Tom: That still doesn't answer the lady's question.

Murt: Very well then. My name is Murt Glug and I came for my wife that's standing over there.

(Points at Tessie).

Mary: Your wife? Tessie?

Bessie: She's fainted. Help me somebody please.

(Tom catches her as she is about to fall and together with Moon helps her to chair).

Mary: Water quickly.

(Mrs Black locates water).

Mary: Help her to her room with me Tom.

(All go off with Tessie except Moon, Glug and Bessie).

Bessie: (To Glug) You got my message?

Murt: 'Twas given to me.

Bessie: I didn't think she'd react like that. I'm sorry. The shock was too much for her.

(Bessie follows the others. Glug makes for the door. Tom returns).

Tom: Hold on there. What's your hurry?

Moon: Ask him if he'd fancy a cup of tea.

Tom: Will you drink a mouthful of tea?

Murt: I'll drink it out of my hand, standing. I won't sit.

(Tom gets mug of tea).

Moon: My name is Moon, Theophilus Moon, and this gentleman is Tom Shaun Shea and you are the one and only Murt Glug. Right?

Murt: Bullseye.

Tom: You made a right heims of that situation my friend.

Murt: I done my best.

Moon: You call that your best with a sack of hay and a whip instead of a nice bunch of flowers. And that coat! There's enough manure plastered on it to fertilise a small garden. And look at your jaw! There must be a fortnight's beard on it. There's enough dirt in your ears to fill a flower pot. No woman could be expected to endure the likes of you.

Tom: He's right my friend. Every word of what he says is the truth.

Moon: The first thing you do when you meet a lady is take off your hat.

(Moon takes off Glug's hat and is almost overcome by the smell. Drops it on the floor. Walks around Glug the better to survey him).

Moon: How long since you combed your hair or washed it? How long since you blew your nose? You drink your tea like a horse drinking water. You smell of cowdung and pony dung, sour milk and pigswill. Man dear you're a walking dungheap.

Tom: He's being cruel to be kind Murt. You'll never get her to go back with you as you are now.

Murt: What can I do?

Tom: You could start by having a bath.

Moon: Not yet. He's not ready for a bath yet, not until he's steeped and fully steeped and steeped again after that.

Tom: Steeped?

Moon: Aye steeped. The tide is out. The place for him now is up to his adam's apple in the pool in the black rocks. Let him steep there till the tide returns in the evening. That should soften his hide for a hot seaweed bath at

Maggie Daly's. There's no other way you'll get the dirt off him.

Tom: Are you willing to give it a try?

Murt: Would I have to strip?

Tom: Aye.

Murt: To the skin?

Tom: To the skin.

Moon: Like the day you were born my friend. That pelt of yours has two inches of concentrated dirt on it. There's no other way. Everything must come off.

Tom: You'll want a new suit of clothes, a dandy hat, a shirt.

Moon: And boots, don't forget new boots.

Tom: Have you the price of all these?

Murt: I have.

Tom: You're sure.

Murt: I am.

Moon: This is your first step on the road to conversion. Now for the black rocks to put him steeping. Lead on Tom. *(Exit Tom and Glug)* I wouldn't be a fish in the Atlantic Ocean this evening if you gave me my weight in gold.

(Picks up hat and throws it out the door. Exit Moon).

CURTAIN
for end of Scene 3, Act 3.

ACT THREE

Scene Four

Afternoon of the following day — the last day. Moon removing picture from wall. Tom enters with bags. There are several bags and trunks already deposited in kitchen. Tom drags trunk nearer exit.

Moon: Do you want a hand with that?

Tom: No need. All Mary O'Dea's personal belongings are contained in here so you might say 'tis a labour of love.

Moon: A job you want to do yourself.

Tom: Exactly. You took the words out of my mouth.

Moon: The last day Tom.

Tom: You're in a pensive mood my friend.

Moon: Bare walls Tom. Bare as a barn in the full flush of summer. Still I suppose everything must run its true course and all good times come to an end. I should thank God for giving me the grace to be able to see such things in a true light.

Tom: It wonder if anyone outside of this house knows what's happening here today.

Moon: It's nobody else's concern Tom. It affects only us.

Tom: But it's the last chapter in a book that was started a long, long time ago. You'd think somebody would want to know how it all ended.

Moon: Our story is told Tom and all the characters disposed of. Time now for a new book to begin. Time for a new species, strong, rough and ready, hungry for change, impatient for the passing of all we once held so dear. Time to move over Tom. We're standing in the way.

Tom: Yes. We had our turn you might say. Things must

change. That's life.

Moon: What about the furniture?

Tom: All sold in bulk to a secondhand dealer. He'll collect it when we're gone.

Moon: Hard to believe we'll never see this place again Tom.

Tom: Like you said it's time to move over. My father used always say . . . he used always say . . .

Moon: What did he say Tom?

Tom: I've forgotten.

Moon: What would you say yourself? That's the important thing.

Tom: I would say we had good times here Moon. Times that won't come again. What will you do with yourself? You have made plans naturally?

Moon: I have a sister in Dublin. She's invited me to stay with her.

Tom: You'll be sure to come to our place for your holidays next summer.

Moon: That's a promise.

Tom: No man could ever be more welcome. You're coming to the wedding of course.

Moon: Oh yes. Mary's asked me. A month from today isn't it?

Tom: A month from today. Did I ever think in my wildest dreams I'd have her for a wife.

Moon: If any man deserves her Tom you're that man.
(Enter Dolly wearing coat, cap and carrying handbag).

Tom: Where are you off to?

Dolly: Con and Molly Somers are nowhere to be found. My mother's worried. The bus leaves in fifteen minutes and if I don't find them it'll go without them.

Tom: Off with you then and don't dilly-dally or 'twill go without you too.
(Exit Dolly).

Moon: I said it before Tom and I'll say it again. There's

86

something fishy about Con and Molly Somers.

Tom: Like what?

Moon: I don't know what. Just a nagging suspicion that something's radically wrong in that particular quarter. *(Tom exits through door with bag. Enter Widows and Nixes, dressed to leave).*

Moon: Well ladies the time has come. Very soon the last surviving Buds of Ballybunion will be transported forever from this place and our likes will never pass this way again. A historical occasion surely.

Bessie: And nobody knows Mr Moon. Nobody cares. It's as though we never existed.

(Enter Mary carrying another suitcase. She hands it to Tom who has re-entered. He takes it out).

Mary: Oh dear! I don't know whether to laugh or cry.

Moon: I wouldn't cry Mary, not with your wedding day round the corner.

Mary: I'll miss you Mr Moon. I'll miss all of you. *(Re-enter Tom).* Tom I've been meaning to ask you. Whatever happened to Mr Glug?

Tom: He'll be alright. He's around somewhere.

Moon: Re-creating himself.

Mary: You're sure he's not gone for good?

Moon: No. He'll be back. You might say he's been overhauled and that he's waiting for a favourable tide. Would you agree Tom?

Tom: Aye. He should be ready to slip his moorings any time now. We should see a new vessel altogether.

Moon: Properly steeped eh Tom?

Tom: Aye Moon, properly steeped.

(Enter Dolly).

Dolly: They're coming. Con and Molly.

Mary: Well that's one worry set aside.

(Enter Con and Molly, ushered in by Fr Bunce).

Mary: We were beginning to get worried. The bus leaves in

less than a quarter of an hour.

Con: Sorry Mary. It couldn't be helped. We were unavoidably delayed.

Fr Bunce: My dear friends I would ask you to pay attention for a moment or two. Con here has something to say to you.

Con: What I have to say grieves me deeply but it must be said. We have deceived you all, Molly and I.

All: No! No! Never! *(General remarks).*
(Molly bursts into tears).

Con: I'm afraid it's too true. We have deceived each and every one of you but worst of all we have dishonoured this house.

Mary: But how? What have you done that's so awful.

Molly: We're not married.

Mary: What did you say?

Molly: We're not married. *(Starts to cry).*

Moon: You're not married!

Con: What she means is we're married alright but not to each other.

Mary: Oh my God and to think you used this house for your goings on!

Mrs Black: Adulteration is the vilest of all the sins.

Moon: How do you know?

Mrs Bunce: Had you no shame, either one of you?

Con: Oh we had. We were never without it. We knew we were living a lie, that we would have to pay the price, that this moment would come sooner or later. It was always there.

Mrs Black: And you, you common hussy. What have you to say for yourself?

Con: She's no hussy. I won't have you call her that.

Mrs Black: And what else is she that bed-rolled and adulterated without a licence from God nor man? No wonder this house is closing down. There won't be luck or grace under the roof of it from this day forward.

Mrs Bunce: And you the whole cause. Suppose we all behaved like you.

Moon: It wouldn't have done you one bit of harm.

Mrs Bunce: Silence you. This house was doomed from the minute she started her shenanigans. Is it a woman that never wore a corset. . .

Mrs Black: Going around without a corset is as bad as going naked.

Mrs Bunce: 'Tis a wonder a bolt of lightning didn't strike the roof or a tidal wave take us under.

Mrs Black: Once a whorehouse, always a whorehouse.

Tom: See here now! That's not fair. There's no call for talk like that.

Mrs Bunce: The truth will be told.

Fr Bunce: That's enough mother and you Mrs Black, apologise this instant to Mary O'Dea. This minute, do you hear? Say you're sorry — this very minute. Come on.

Mrs Black: Sorry.

Fr Bunce: Louder.

Mrs Black: Sorry.

Fr Bunce: Now sit the pair of you and let's hear no more from either one of you.

Mary: How long has this been going on?

Con: Thirty years.

Moon: You mean all that time you've been. . .

Tom: What about your wife?

Con: She's dead these ten years.

Tom: Eh!

Mary: And you Molly. Your husband?

Molly: He's dead too.

Mary: But when they were alive you came here to this house, masquerading as man and wife and afterwards when they were dead why didn't you marry?

89

Con: Our children wouldn't hear of it. They kept us apart, deliberately.

Molly: They said we'd bring disgrace on them.

Con: Young people think they have a monopoly on love.

Molly: I'm sorry Mary.

Mrs Black: Sorry she says. Sorry for decorating this good Catholic home. Sorry for making a Sodom and Goodmorrah out of Ballybunion.

Fr Bunce: Mrs Black where's your charity?

Mrs Black: (To Molly) Go long you, you porsatute you!

Con: God's sake were none of you ever in love? Did none of you ever know the agony of wanting someone? D'you know what it is to be apart hour after hour, day after day, year after year with the heart withering all the time, longing for the fall of the year and the blessed month of September?

Tom: You kept this inside you for thirty years?

Con: Thirty years Tom.

Mary: I can't believe it Molly. You're just not the type.

Molly: We were childhood sweethearts Mary but Con had to go to America because he couldn't find work here. It was a bad time there too. Things didn't work out for him. Then a year passed without a word, then another and I thought he had forgotten.

Con: I didn't make it over there. I decided I was no good for her so I worked my passage to Australia. I did well. I came home to find she was married. I took a wife and I prospered but one day . . . one day you see . . .

Tom: Go on Con.

Con: One day I came here to Ballybunion with my family and I saw her. I kept well away. She was with him. After a while he lay back on the strand and she went walking along the shore. I followed. She went further and further from the crowd. I still followed. Then she turned and just like that we fell into each other's arms. That was where it all began thirty years ago. As the tide was turning we fell for the first time.

Mrs Black: And this is where it ends after thirty years of carnivorous knowledge.

Tom: No, it needn't end here. You're free to marry and you still love each other. Never mind your children. They've grown up now. It's time you thought of yourselves. You've suffered long enough.

Mrs Bunce: If that's what you call suffering may God forgive us all.

Fr Bunce: May God forgive us all indeed but not for your reasons mother.

Moon: May God forgive us all for being so hard on Con and Molly Somers when they want our help — and I can tell you this — if the priest won't marry them on the same day as Tom Shaun and Mary O'Dea, be Janey, but I'll do it myself!

Fr Bunce: Don't worry Mr Moon — I'll marry them on the same day I marry Tom Shaun and Mary O'Dea. And now mother I have something to say to you. I'm in line for a parish — God knows not out of turn and I'll be looking for a housekeeper.

Mrs Bunce: A . . . A housekeeper did you say?

Fr Bunce: Of course the kind of housekeeper I have in mind will not be a person who condemns others; will not be a person who cannot forgive and will not be a person who holds a grudge.

Mrs Bunce: Oh, I never hold grudges.

Mrs Black: No. No. She never holds grudges. *(Nudges Mrs Bunce).*

Mrs Bunce: I'll need help.

Fr Bunce: Help?

Mrs Bunce: Somebody to make the beds, wash the dishes, answer the door.

Fr Bunce: Very well you can have Mrs Black if you wish.

Would that be suitable?

Mrs Black: Oh yes, that would be the answer to all our prayers.

Mrs Bunce: Praise be to God.

Mrs Black: Praise be to God.

Fr Bunce: Alright. That much is settled. Now make your overtures to Con and Molly and if I ever catch either of you again without forgiveness in your hearts it's back to the daughters-in-law with the pair of you.

(They rush to make amends).

Mrs Black: Every day's joy to the two of you.

Mrs Bunce: And happiness.

Molly: The two of you will come to the wedding?

Mrs Black: It wouldn't be there without us.

Mrs Bunce: Forgive me Con.

Con: Of course. Of course. No blame to you Mrs Bunce.

(Enter Murt Glug resplendent in new, gaudy, ill-fitting clothes. He carries a bunch of flowers, plucked from the wayside. He advances to Tessie. All are spellbound).

Murt: I'd like for you to give it a second try, it don't mean you must sleep in my bed and it don't mean you have to stay. All it means is that you put me on trial for a while and I'll accept whatever judgement you deliver. *(Tessie is speechless)* Bring Bessie with you. She can stay forever if she wants or she can marry from my house whenever she chooses, if she chooses. So long as you come yourself I don't care who comes.

Tessie: I don't know what to say. I'm in a daze.

Murt: When you don't know what to say the best thing is to say nothing at all and 'twill be said of its own good time.

Tessie: Thank you for the flowers.

Murt: You're welcome. If Bessie was to come and live with us your brother Font would have a free hand. He deserves that poor devil. He's waited long enough. Time now for him to be happy ever after as the saying goes.

Tessie: Would you have a bath every day?

Murt: For what?

Tessie: For me.

Murt: Alright but 'twill have to be in the river till I throw some sort of a bathroom together.

Tessie: And would you comb your hair?

Murt: For why? For why?

Tessie: For me.

Murt: Alright.

Tessie: Every day?

Murt: Alright.

Tessie: And will you use deodorant?

Murt: What's that?

Moon: Eau de Cologne.

Murt: Odey who?

Tom: Toilet water. Body perfume.

Murt: Ah! You mean stink?

Tom: Yes. Stink.

Murt: Stink is for women.

Tessie: Will you do it for me?

Murt: Alright I'll do it for you but wouldn't I always have done anything in this world for you. All I ever knew about women was what I read in the catechism. I'd have done anything you ever asked.

Tessie: Well I've asked you now.

Murt: And I've give you my promise and I say to you come home with me and I'll be the very man you want me to be.

Tessie: You ... You won't expect too much ... in the beginning?

Murt: I'll expect nothing but for you to be around the house.

Tessie: Alright so. I'll give it a try.

(Murt gives a roar of delight and embraces Tessie. All

move off to left except Fr Bunce).

Fr Bunce: And so dearly beloved brethren it came to pass
that on the thirtieth day of September in the year of Our
Lord, nineteen hundred and forty-five, the last remaining Buds of Ballybunion foregathered at Mary O'Dea's
for the final exodus from this radiant and well-beloved
resort. Without fuss, bustle, ostentation or outward
display of emotion they vacated the scene they cherished
for so long. No tear, no sign, no lamentation whatsoever
marked their departure. Neither drum nor trumpet was
sounded as they withdrew to fade forever into the
treasury of thing past.

*(All emerge from house, burdened with bags. Boozer
Malone is last).*
Mary sings:

I walk along a sandy shore beside a silver sea,
Where every wave and ripple there remind me love of
    thee.
And when at night the stars are bright beside the pale
    moon's glow,
I'll dream of Ballybunion and the Buds of long ago.

All sing as they waltz.

Goodbye to Ballybunion where the green seas ebb and
    flow,
Goodbye to every lofty cliff and golden sands below.
Farewell, farewell my only love, the time has come to go,
Goodbye to Ballybunion and the Buds of long ago.

All trip off to the music of Patsy Healy.

FINAL CURTAIN

MORE PLAYS

by

JOHN B. KEANE

BIG MAGGIE
THE CHANGE IN MAME FADDEN
THE CRAZY WALL
THE FIELD
THE MAN FROM CLARE
MOLL
THE YEAR OF THE HIKER
VALUES

SOME BOOKS

by

JOHN B. KEANE

LETTERS OF A SUCCESSFUL T.D.
LETTERS OF AN IRISH PARISH PRIEST
LETTERS OF A MATCHMAKER
LETTERS OF A LOVE-HUNGRY FARMER
LETTERS OF AN IRISH MINISTER OF STATE
LETTERS OF AN IRISH PUBLICAN
LETTERS OF A COUNTRY POSTMAN
LETTERS OF A CIVIC GUARD
STRONG TEA
UNLAWFUL SEX AND OTHER TESTY MATTERS

THE GENTLE ARE OF MATCHMAKING...
IS THE HOLY GHOST REALLY A KERRYMAN?...
SELF PORTRAIT